When It Rains

T.K. Chapin

The Potter's House

When it Rains

T.K. CHAPIN

Potter's House

ISBN: 978-1980762751

DEDICATION

Dedicated to my loving wife.

For all the years she has put up with me

And many more to come.

CONTENTS

ACKNOWLEDGMENTS

First and foremost, I want to thank God. God's salvation through the death, burial and resurrection of Jesus Christ gives us all the ability to have a personal relationship with the creator of the Universe.

I also want to thank my wife. She's my muse and my inspiration. A wonderful wife, an amazing mother and the best person I have ever met. She's great and has always stood by me with every decision I have made along life's way.

I'd like to thank my editors and early readers for helping me along the way. I also want to thank all of my friends and extended family for the support. It's a true blessing to have every person I know in my life.

.

PROLOGUE-HANNAH

FAITH IS EASY WHEN LIFE is going in a direction you want. However, when life throws a curve ball at your head and it's going ninety miles an hour, faith is a different story. My story is the second of these, and it all started when I found out my husband, Jonathan, had been living a double life. Those business trips twice a month down to Florida weren't business at all. It was to see his other wife and children. This was only the beginning of a series of events that were too much for my heart to handle on its own. I needed God. I firmly believe that faith in God can only work when we find the end of ourselves.

It's when one's back is against the red sea and there doesn't seem to be a way out, that God shows up.

When It Rains

CHAPTER 1-HANNAH

"I'M PREGNANT." TWO WORDS, ONE PHRASE that contains the power to change lives. Words that shape entire lives and words that can bring a grown man to his knees. They can bring immense joy or deep sorrow to the soul. When my young, sweet sixteen-year-old, Kayla, uttered those very words two years after my divorce with her father, I knew our lives were about to change again.

Her boyfriend, Matt, whom she had been dating the last two years, was sitting beside her on my old red cross-stitched couch I had picked up at the Goodwill back when we'd first moved out of Jonathan's house. They sat huddled together, and he had one arm around her shoulders, trying to provide her with comfort as they awaited my response.

I was speechless. *How could I let this happen?* I wondered as the guilt weighed on my shoulders. She was my responsibility, and her actions were a direct reflection of my choices. It was a truth that hurt, but I couldn't get around it no matter how badly I didn't want to admit it.

After a long, awkward silence loomed in the air, Matt adjusted on the couch and brought his hands together in his lap. Then, with the utmost confidence, he spoke. "Miss Bates, I want you to know we're keeping it. I already have a job at Subway, and they said they can give me a few more hours."

This child's words highlighted his immaturity and lack of understanding of reality. He knew nothing of what raising a child took. He was merely a child himself. He appeared to see this child

5

growing inside my daughter as just a budgetary concern, but Matt was just a kid. I didn't expect him to understand something that even most adults nowadays can't fully comprehend when they first embark on the journey of parenthood.

Still without speaking, I stood up from my recliner.

Venturing into the kitchenette of the apartment, I refilled my cup of coffee as I still tried to wrap my head around the fact that my little girl was pregnant. Kayla, my perfect little innocent angel, had lost her wings. Where did my little girl who'd made mud pies outside in the dirt and came to me when she got hurt go?

Kayla stood up from the couch and came to the counter that separated the kitchen from the living room, her eyes wide. "Mom? Can you please say something?"

Turning to her, I carefully set my cup of coffee down on the counter and peered into her eyes. Worry weighed heavily in her eyes. I suspected she wanted me to kiss the situation and make it all better, but this wasn't just a little scratch on her knee and she wasn't five years old.

Reality began to sink into my bones. Tears welled in my eyes as I saw not just my daughter standing on the other side of the counter, but a scared and frightened mother-to-be.

"Matt." My gaze caught his. "You need to leave now so I can speak to my daughter alone, please."

He stood up and headed for the door. Kayla rushed to his side and pulled his arm, trying to stop him from leaving. "Don't leave, Matt! This is your baby too!"

Pausing, he looked at me, and then at my daughter. "Maybe you should listen to your mom now. Not listening to her is how we ended up here."

Kayla's shoulders drooped as she let go of his arm. Reluctantly, she walked by his side to the door and paused as she turned to me. "Can I walk him to his car?"

"It's raining."

"I can put a coat on."

"If you must."

As the door shut, I sighed heavily and pressed my hand against my brow as the pent-up tears streamed down my cheeks. *How could I have let this happen?* Maybe if I hadn't taken the last two years to focus on myself and my healing from the divorce with Jonathan, things would be different. Maybe if I'd paid a little more attention to her instead of going to all of those support groups at the church for counseling, my daughter wouldn't be pregnant.

Taking my cup of coffee with a side of guilt, I returned to my recliner in the living room. I tried to formulate in my mind how to break *my* news to her. There had been an idea tossing back and forth in my mind for the last two and a half months. Up until now, I wasn't sure if it would be good for the two of us. Tonight's news concreted my decision. Yes, my daughter would be upset with me, especially now, but it'd be for the best.

She came back into the apartment, a coldness in the air with her as she entered the living room and sat down on the couch once more, her wet coat soaking through the sofa.

"We're moving." Two words, one phrase that contains the power to change lives.

CHAPTER 2-HANNAH

HER BEDROOM DOOR SLAMMED SHUT

moments later. A cringe of pain rippled through me as I empathized with the pain she must have been feeling in the moment. She didn't understand it now, but she would with time. Picking up my cell phone, I called Luke, the man I had spoken with on the phone a few times about his father, who needed a caretaker. He had made me an offer, but I hadn't given him my decision yet. That was two months ago. I had found the opening through an online bulletin board requesting someone to come live with his father, Mac, on a ranch in Eastern Washington. The job entailed cooking meals, buying groceries, and keeping the house clean. In exchange, we'd have a guest house to live in and a monthly salary.

T.K. Chapin

"I'll do it."

"Hannah?"

"Yes, it's me. The caretaker position for your father. If the offer is still available, I'll take it."

"That's great! I was starting to wonder if I'd hear from you again."

"I guess I just needed God to confirm it for me somehow. Tonight, he did."

"I love it when God makes it easy like that. When can you get here?"

"Next week."

"I'll let Mac know tomorrow when I go out there, and we'll be looking forward to your arrival."

Hearing my daughter's door creak open, I said

my goodbyes. "Looking forward to it. I'll be in touch."

I hung up my call, and Kayla walked out into the living room. Her eyes were red and swollen. Wandering over to the couch, she dropped onto it in a dramatic fashion. Clutching the couch pillow against her stomach, she stared at the ceiling. "Mom. Can we please just stay here? It's not like I can get more pregnant if we stay. I'm sorry. I know you're disappointed in me, and I am too . . . but moving isn't going to help anything. Please, Mom?"

I shook my head. "I know you don't understand, but the answer is no. I am the parent, and you are the child. The decision is final."

"That's so unfair!" she screamed.

Closing my eyes, I reached down deep inside to

draw strength from the Spirit of God to sustain me. "Kayla. You cannot speak to me that way. We are moving and there is no changing that."

She shook her head. "You find out I'm pregnant and then you get back at me by moving us. You're a horrible person! It all makes sense now. Why Dad left you for her."

Her words sliced through layers of healing and stung a sensitive part of my heart. I had to remind myself that she was only a child, and she was trying to hurt me because she was hurt. She didn't mean it. I wished she didn't know any of the details of the divorce, but she wasn't a small child when it all happened two years ago. She was there, sitting on the stairs in the living room when Brenda, Jonathan's other wife, called and told me about their family. She was there when Jonathan kissed her goodbye and moved to Florida. I've never hated a person, but Jonathan was right there on the cusp for what he did to Kayla by choosing his other family.

"I'm going to call Matt's parents and try to figure out how we are all going to parent this new baby coming into the world in nine months."

Shaking her head, she said, "You wouldn't tell them."

I stood up. "His mother goes to our church. Why wouldn't I tell them? They need to know our children are having a child, and we have to decide how we are going to raise it, especially in light of our moving."

"You know his dad beats him! Why are you trying to ruin everything? I hate you so much!" With that, she stormed out of the room and down the hallway. The door slammed once again. How did my sweet, easygoing little girl turn into such an angry and hurtful child? My heart felt a twinge thinking of her father, Jonathan. I didn't miss him, but I did miss Kayla having a father figure in the home.

Scrolling through my phone, I landed on Carla's name. She was Matt's mother. I pondered the easiest way to proceed that didn't get Matthew harmed. I was upset with Matthew for impregnating my daughter, but I didn't want him hurt.

CHAPTER 3-HANNAH

I ARRANGED FOR COFFEE AT a local coffee shop downtown the next afternoon with Carla. The kids were in school, and I had a bit of time to process the idea of my daughter being pregnant. Though I wasn't thrilled my sixteen-year-old was pregnant, I did understand it was done and over with and it was time to prepare for a baby. Things needed to be sorted out between the grownups.

Sitting down at the table, I took a drink of my coffee.

"Wow. You seem so nervous, Hannah."

"Sorry," I said, setting my cup down. "It's kind of a huge deal."

Carla shifted in her seat, appearing

uncomfortable as she sat across from me. She shook her head, rubbing the corner of her cup with a thumb. "What's going on?"

"I don't know how to be delicate with this, but basically, our children are pregnant."

"Excuse me?" she asked, pulling back. "No." She adjusted in her seat, leaning slightly forward across the table as her eyes widened. "What?"

"Kayla is pregnant."

"Um."

"I know. I was devastated too."

Letting out a sigh, she looked away from me. With an air of condemnation toward me, she said, "I knew that Kayla was a bad seed."

"Excuse me? Your son impregnated her! It takes

two!"

"I heard about Jonathan and his whole other wife and family in Florida, Hannah. I'm sure that's been hard on you and it's caused you to slack in your parenting. I get that, but now my son's life is ruined because of your daughter not being able to keep her morals intact."

My heart splintered. "How could you bring up my divorce? You're blaming that for your son getting my daughter pregnant? Unbelievable."

Crossing my arms, anger seethed within me. Sure, Kayla was to blame, but so was Matt. This coffee with a friend was turning into a battle of whose fault it was instead of thinking of the future.

"No, no. Honey. I'm not saying your divorce caused it to happen. Just the fact that they've had plenty of opportunity at your house to commit acts. I'm *always* home. It never happened at my house, I can assure you of that!"

Standing up, I shook my head as my heart was broken by someone I thought was a friend. "Your son's precious life doesn't have to be ruined, *Carla*. I really wanted to try co-parenting with you, but now I see that isn't possible. Maybe you can have him give up his rights. We're moving next week to Washington State. Call me if you talk him into it."

I walked out and left my almost full coffee and my old friend behind.

CHAPTER 4-HANNAH

THE NEXT WEEK WAS A smudge of ink smeared on the calendar as I counted the days, hours, and minutes until we would finally leave the city of Flagstaff, Arizona. I was done with the people, done with the drama, and ready for a fresh start in a new place.

Loading the final box into the smallest sized U-Haul truck, we shut the door and proceeded to hook up the car trailer to pull behind us. We, along with the youth group from our church, had finished loading by seven in the morning, an impressive feat for my daughter and me, who loved sleep more than anything else in life.

"You could've just let me drive the car." Kayla's words were under her breath as we were struggling to latch the trailer onto the back of the U-Haul as the youth drank the refreshments we had out for them.

Pausing, I looked up at her. "Yeah, but then we couldn't have fun talking all the way there."

"Oh, yeah. Lots of fun."

After we got the car up onto the trailer, we thanked the youth group and then we got into the cab of the U-Haul, setting out for the open road.

We were two hours into our drive when Kayla pulled out her ear buds and put them in the front pocket of her backpack. Turning to me, she said, "Mom?"

"Yeah, dear?"

"I'm sorry about the other day."

Without her detailing what she was apologizing for, I knew it was for the behavior on the night when she and Matt broke the news to me about her pregnancy. She wasn't happy about leaving Matt and her friends behind in Arizona, but I knew she was realizing quickly that I was the only person in the world she'd know in Washington.

"I forgive you. Hey, do you want to put on that CD that Matt gave you?"

"No, not really." Her gaze turned out the window. "Tell me about this Mac guy we're going to be sharing a house with."

I laughed. "We're not sharing a house with him. We'll have our own quarters in the ranch's guest house. He's old, I know that much. Oh, and very grumpy."

23

"Is he like a cowboy?"

I shrugged. "I don't know much about him."

"Does he have internet?"

"I'm not sure."

"These are important things to know, Mom. He could be a serial killer with no internet, and we're just going to live with him? Really safe, Mom. Jeez."

Smiling, I shook my head. "You worry too much. It's going to be a good change. After all you and I have been through these last two years since Dad left, I think it's overdue."

She got really quiet. Which wasn't a surprise to me. She didn't like talking about Jonathan. It hurt too much for her to dwell on her father. I didn't blame her for that. I couldn't imagine the torment her soul was still going through with the fact that he had picked the other family over ours. Picked his other children over her. He promised to visit her a lot when he moved to Florida after the divorce, but she had only seen him once since he'd left. She needed her father, and his actions showed he couldn't possibly care less. It broke my heart to see my little girl struggle without having a father in her life. No child deserves to be without a father.

"Where are we stopping tonight again?" she asked a few minutes later.

"Idaho Falls, Idaho."

CHAPTER 5- LUKE

CHANGING THE BLOODIED GAUZE FROM my father's leg wound, I winced at the sight. He was too old to keep getting hurt like this. He had fallen down again, this time outside, right off the front porch. He had cataracts and couldn't see very well. Mac had lain in the dirt for three hours until I just happened to come out and visit him. If I hadn't been there, he would have certainly bled out.

My father was a hard man to live with growing up. He suffered from PTSD in the Korean War and self-medicated with whiskey for most of my life. It wasn't until the summer of 2009 after losing his wife, Rita, my mom, to breast cancer that he finally put the bottle away. I was already grown and had already learned from him what not to do and what kind of man I never wanted to become.

"You could be a little gentler, sonny boy," he said as I redressed his wound.

"Yeah, and you could be a little less stubborn and take the cell phone I bought you months ago."

"I don't need technology. I've lived a full life without it." Pushing himself up, he leaned against the wall his bed was set against in his bedroom.

The bedroom, along with the rest of the house, was made of oak. The oak was logged from up on the hill just a few miles away on another patch of land he owned.

Taking the remnants of trash from the nightstand, I left the bedroom and went down the hall. Pictures of Victor, Mom, Dad, and me lined each wall, highlighting our family from a different time in our life. The pictures that hung on the wall told a different story from what my brother or I would tell. Pictures in front of the church on Easter didn't show my father's hangover from the night before. The pictures only caught glimmers of the surface, nothing below. I hardly ever stopped in the hall and looked at any of them, with the exception of the one of my mother at the far end. I missed her. It was of her and us boys. I was twelve at the time, Victor just over six, and she looked happy.

Arriving in the kitchen, I opened the cupboard below the sink and tossed the garbage away.

My phone rang in my pocket and I pulled it out.

It was Victor.

"Hey. How is he today?"

"He's grumpy, as usual."

He laughed. "When's that woman getting there?"

"Hannah is arriving tomorrow sometime." Crossing the kitchen floor, I went over to the table and sat down, looking out at the field where cows used to graze. I longed for the time I didn't have to continuously check up on my dad's wellbeing.

"Did you warn the gal about Dad?"

"Of course. I already feel bad enough for the gal. She has a daughter coming with her too. On the phone, she told me that her husband left her a couple of years back. She's had a rough go of it, so this might be a good thing for her, like it will be for us, not having to come check on him."

"Tread carefully, brother. Sounds like she's damaged goods, and I know how you like to be a knight."

"Don't be crass."

After getting off the phone with Victor, I walked out the back door and went over to the fence. The sun was just starting to set, and I took in the beauty of the array of colors painted in the sky. Leaning against the white-washed boards of the fence, I clasped my hands together and bowed my head in prayer.

"God, please let this woman and her daughter work out. I know my dad is a jerk, but he needs to see Your love again in his life. He needs Your love to soften his heart before the end comes. If You can find it in Your will for this to happen, it'd be greatly appreciated. Amen."

CHAPTER 6-HANNAH

AFTER CHECKING INTO OUR HOTEL in Idaho Falls, Kayla and I ventured across the street to stretch our legs. As we journeyed down the walking path along the river, we could see the Mormon temple across the river. It stood taller than the hotels or any of the other buildings along the river and looked to be crafted with a detail unmatched by anything I'd seen before.

"What religion is that for?" Kayla asked, pointing it out.

"Mormon."

"Oh. Elise from school was a Mormon. They're Christian, right?"

"Some might be, but their doctrines are not

31

Christian. They don't believe in the same Jesus as we do. They believe He is separate from God, not in the trinity. There's a lot more differences between Biblical Christianity and Mormons. I actually have a book in one of my boxes if you really want to know more."

She shook her head. "That's okay . . ." Looking around, and then forward, she said softly, "I miss my friends."

Stopping, I turned to her and grabbed both of her hands in mine. Peering into her eyes as the soft sound of the falls were only a few steps further up the path, I wanted to assure her of the future. "I know you have a lot of pain inside right now. Lots of hormones whooshing around, lots of confusion too, and I appreciate your doing your best to seem okay, Kayla."

"Okay." Her word was soft, but the pain could be heard in the tone.

I continued. "Life is going to get better for you, Kayla. I know you miss Matt, and I know you're hurting because of it, and moving away from all of your friends is hard, but I promise things will work out. God has a plan for you, Daughter."

"It's just so hard to believe that when my life is a train wreck, Mom." She started to lightly cry, and her hand found her belly. "I'm only sixteen and I'm pregnant. I have to go start in a new school, and everyone is going to make fun of me and stare at me."

"Would you rather do your schooling online and at home?"

Her eyes widened. "You'd let me do that?"

"Absolutely. I couldn't imagine going to a school, let alone a new school, pregnant and sixteen. I'm here to help you."

She frowned, then smiled, and frowned again. Then she stepped toward me and hugged me. It was the perfect hug in a moment of uncertainty as we were halfway between our old life and our new one in Washington.

There was no way to know for certain how the future would go for the two of us, but I knew God was with us and He was watching out not only for our wellbeing, but for our hearts too. God knew that hug was exactly what I needed. God's love for me overwhelmed my emotions as Kayla hugged me. My eyes watered.

Wiping our eyes, we continued onward to the

falls. Coming up a slope of cement, we arrived at a metal railing. The falls were about three feet in height and tumbled lightly over and into the water. They weren't impressive enough to justify a name for a town in my mind, but they were pretty, I guess.

"Mom?" she said, as we held onto the railing, looking out at the falls.

"Yeah?"

"These are the '*majestic falls*'?" she asked, a laugh to her tone as she did.

Smiling, I laughed. "I guess so."

CHAPTER 7-LUKE

I'D TRADED IN MY COWBOY boots for dress shoes a long time ago and became an investment banker at *Young's* in Spokane. Essentially, I helped businesses make a lot of money. Whether it was buying up other companies and dissolving them or raising funds for an upcoming research and development, I'm the guy people called when they were ready to make a big decision, and I never made mistakes.

"Corey, calm down." Standing up with Corey Saks in my ear piece, I walked over to the window of my office and looked down upon the cars driving the street below. Corey Saks was the owner of *Bing Bong Toy Company* who had just received their quarterly reports and found out they're down three-quarters of a percent because of new business that was gobbling up a portion of the toy market with a new product. "Listen, this is what we do. We buy them out."

"But that's no small amount of money, Luke!"

"Neither is the loss here in the long run. The board will approve it. I'm telling you it's the right move."

He took a deep breath. "Okay. I'll talk to the board and let you know."

"Remember to breathe, Corey."

He laughed. "I know, I know. Thanks."

Hanging up the call, I walked over to my bookshelf and picked up my baseball. It was the baseball I had hit in my college days, senior year, to be exact. I'd slugged it out of the field and closed out

our undefeated season. A proud moment for myself.
Tossing it up, I caught it and walked with it over to
my desk. Pressing my desk phone's button to reach
Cindy, my receptionist, I said, "Hold my calls. I'm
taking an early lunch today."

"Pamela called again. You're going to have to
talk to her, Luke."

Ignoring her, I asked, "So, can you hold my
calls?"

"Yes."

"Thanks."

Leaving my baseball on my desk, I grabbed my
jacket from the back of my chair and headed out to
grab a bite at my favorite place down the block—
Antonio's, a hole in the wall Mexican restaurant
with the best *Carne Asada* steak burrito in town.

As I walked down the sidewalk outside the high rise of my office, my cell phone rang.

It was my dad's new resident, Hannah.

I answered the call via my Bluetooth device in my ear. "How's the road trip going?"

"It's all right. I'm a couple of hours out of town. Can you meet me there, or does Mac know about us showing up with a U-Haul?"

Checking my watch, I said, "He knows about you. Just go knock on the front door and introduce yourself, then start unloading your stuff into the guest house. I'll be out there this evening to make sure everything is okay. I wanted to come sooner and help, but I have a meeting I can't get out of. Some people from the church out there will be there to help unload as soon as Mac tells them you are there."

"Oh, wow. Really? That wasn't needed. Kayla and I can unload."

"No, no. I told the pastor all about you, and he volunteered the help. These people love new people and helping."

After a moment, she said, "Okay. I can't turn down free help. Thank you."

Arriving at the front door of Antonio's, I paused with my hand on the door. "You're welcome. I'll see you tonight out at the ranch."

CHAPTER 8-HANNAH

SPOTTING THE DRIVEWAY THAT ABRUPTLY dropped off to the right of the road and onto a gravel road under an oak tree, I knew we had arrived. Luke had given me the address along with a note about how it dropped off the road quickly. Suddenly, my stomach jumped into my throat as we started down the bumpy road, the final stretch of our journey.

We passed under the shade of large towering trees covering both sides of the gravel road.

"You okay, Mom?" Kayla asked, noticing my unease.

I nodded. Nothing like a long road trip to rekindle my daughter's fondness for me. While I appreciated her concern about my wellbeing, I

41

couldn't shake the fears that were rising within me.

What if things don't work out? Where would we go?

What if Mac is too mean? What if the guest house is

a junk shack? These were all issues I couldn't let my

daughter worry about.

Then the trees broke away from the road and we

came into a wide-open area. Fields on both sides

and a mountain set not too far in the distance. It was

more beautiful than the pictures online could

capture.

"Look, a mountain!" Kayla said, smiling as she

looked out the passenger window. It was as if she

was ten again and fascinated by the simple things in

life.

I smiled. "Yep, pretty neat, and the neighbor

next door has a horse."

"Can I ride it?"

Shaking my head, I said, "I'm not sure. We'll have to see."

We drove down the gravel crescent-shaped driveway and parked in front of the guest house.

Climbing out of the truck, Kayla said, "I'm going for a walk. I need to move my legs after that long road trip."

"Okay. I'm going to go meet Mac."

Traversing over toward the house, I noticed the sound of crickets humming in the distance as I took in the beauty of the property. This place was going to be a blessing to my daughter and me. I just knew it.

Up on the porch of Mac's house, I opened the

old wooden screen door and gave the door two strong knocks.

Letting loose of the screen, it creaked shut. I turned around and watched Kayla as she stopped at the fence line and peered over at the mountain. I felt that this was the kind of place where a person could reconnect with God and experience the beauty that life has to offer.

A rugged, hoarse voice startled me from behind. "What are you doing on my property? I told you Jehovah's Witnesses to leave me alone!"

Jumping, I quickly turned to see a set of worn eyes looking out through the screen door. He had a head of white hair, but not much of it.

My heart raced.

"Luke didn't tell you about me?"

"Who is *me?*"

"Hannah." Slightly turning toward the yard and fields, I pointed. "And my daughter, Kayla."

"Right. The *help*." He grunted.

He pushed open the screen door and hopped out with his crutches.

"Name's Mac." He extended a hand, his other arm busy holding him up with one crutch.

Reluctantly, I reached a hand out and shook his. "Hannah."

"I know that. You already told me."

Not saying a word, I nodded as I lifted a prayer to God to help me with the fruit of patience in my heart.

"I only have one rule while you live here—don't make me mad or you're outta here. I know my son probably told you I need a lot of help, but I don't. I bathe myself, I clothe myself, and I can cook. You're mostly here to keep an eye on me because I keep having accidents where I fall down. My eyes are bad is all. I'll be done with these crutches once I heal up here shortly. My boys just worry too much about me."

"Okay. Although I would prefer to cook. That way, I earn my keep somehow."

His eyes turned to Kayla at the fence and his face softened for a second before turning hard again. "Fine. That your girl?"

"Yes."

"Where's her father?"

Shaking my head, I glanced down. "Florida."

"That's too bad. I'm sorry to hear that." He turned and headed back inside his house. Stopping, he turned his head and said, "I'll let the pastor know you're here, and he'll head over with the youth to help unload."

"Thank you. I look forward to getting to know you more."

He nodded, then went inside, and I walked out to take in the sights with Kayla.

"Look at that, Mom." She pointed toward the guest house and to what looked to be the remains of a garden of some sort. There were rows of dirt, but they were overgrown with weeds. I'd had a greenhouse and a garden back at the old house with Jonathan. I grew all sorts of fresh vegetables and

47

even a few flowers. I missed the feeling of the soil in my fingers as I planted and tended my garden.

"I wonder when was the last time someone gardened it?" I asked, turning to her to carry on the dialog.

"I'm sure you could turn that heap of old dirt and weeds into something beautiful, Mom. You were so good at it."

I smiled and put my arm around her as we turned back to the fence line and the mountains. "Should we go check out the new digs?"

"Did you just use the word 'digs'?"

We both started to laugh.

CHAPTER 9-HANNAH

KAYLA AND I WERE ABLE to unload boxes until the people from the church arrived at almost four o'clock that afternoon. Walking out from the guest house and on my way back to the U-Haul truck, I saw an old pickup truck driving up the gravel road. Stopping, I shielded my eyes from the sun as I tried to get a good look at who our help would be.

Coming out the front door, Kayla asked, "Did you know there's an attic with a bunch of dusty stuff in there?"

"Oh, cool. Hey, since you're here, come say hello to these people from the church."

"Okay." There was a hint of a whine to her voice, but she obliged. Arriving to my side, she smiled and waved along with me. "How long do I have to hang

49

around?"

Continuing with my smile and wave, I leaned toward her. "Don't start with the attitude. We've had a pleasant time on the road and getting here."

"I just forgot that this is *forever,* and I am mad about it."

The truck pulled up to us and shut off.

Turning to her, I said, "Don't embarrass me. Be nice."

Three guys got out and approached us.

"You must be Hannah and Kayla. I'm Pastor Charlie, and I brought with me some extra hands. Owen and Kirk."

"Nice to meet you." Shaking all of their hands, I glanced at the U-Haul. "There's not a whole lot left, just heavy stuff."

"That's why we're here," Kirk said with a smile as he and Owen walked over and jumped into the back of the moving truck.

"You two relax. We got this," Owen added as he walked by.

Pastor Charlie walked with me toward the guest house.

"I'm going to work on my room." Kayla went in ahead of us, and the pastor stopped short of the front door of the guest house.

Lowering his voice, he said, "What brings you out to our little community besides helping out Mac?"

"Kayla and I needed a new start."

He nodded. "I hope you find what you're looking for out here. You know our church has a great youth group?"

Coming in closer, so Kayla couldn't hear, I said, "I want to get this out now. I know it's forward, but you should know. She's pregnant. Long story. But I'm not sure she'll be too into a youth group for a while."

"Okay, but believe me when I say this—all those teenagers in the youth group are sinners."

We both laughed.

Then he continued. "She's welcome to come regardless of the pregnancy, and I'm sure they'd be happy to have her. If you ever need anything, don't hesitate to call." Handing me a business card for the *Inn at the Lake*, he continued. "That's our residence and our inn my wife and I run."

"Neat! Thank you."

Kirk and Owen were carrying my dresser down the ramp and were approaching us near the door. Kirk asked, "Where to?"

"My room. I'll show you the way."

Charlie went over to the moving truck and I led them inside.

I had them set it directly below the window that pointed toward the mountain. They left the room, and I went over to the boxes in my room near the closet. Opening up the first box, I pulled out a framed picture of Kayla and me when she was only a newborn. I was sitting in the rocking chair beside her crib in her room, and she was asleep on my chest. Jonathan had snapped the picture of the two of us.

Setting the picture frame on the dresser, I thought of Kayla and the baby that was now growing inside her. The future was uncertain for all three of us. I wasn't ready to help my daughter be a mother at this point in my life. My eyes watering, I lowered my head and prayed silently. *God . . . I don't know what You're doing, but if You can shed a little light on the situation, I'd appreciate it.*

"Mom?" My daughter's voice behind me in the doorway brought me out of my prayer. Wiping my eyes, I turned to her.

"Yeah?"

She crossed the wood floor over to me. "Remember this?"

Looking down, I saw a picture of our family

vacation we had taken to the Grand Canyon when she was ten, six years ago. My heart flinched with pain.

"Yeah. That was a fun trip."

The reality was that she didn't understand how much pain was laced within the memories of her father for me. She didn't understand that for every happy memory I had with him, there were three more stories circling nearby that I knew were connected to his other family. The 'emergency' business meeting in Florida halfway through our family vacation wasn't something that Kayla most likely even recalled.

Her eyes were downcast, so I asked, "What's wrong?"

She shook her head.

"You can tell me."

She started to cry. Biting her lip, she sighed. "I know you hate him, but I miss him, Mom."

My heart broke hearing her say it. Pulling her in close, I hugged her tightly. "I know you do, and it's okay to feel that way. Everything is going to be okay, Kayla. God has a plan and is working out things for good. We must wait upon Him and put our trust in Him."

CHAPTER 10-LUKE

PULLING UP BEHIND A SILVER mid-sized sedan, I parked and tossed my Bluetooth into the passenger seat. Peering out the windows, I tried to see if anyone was out and about. Glancing toward the guest house, I took a deep breath as I prayed that my dad wasn't too harsh with her already. The last gal we had out on the ranch didn't last a full forty-eight hours before burning rubber in the middle of the night. My father was resistant to the idea of a caretaker. He'd lived on this ranch for over forty years without a lick of help. I suspected that for him to admit he needed it would be a blow not only to his ego, but to his understanding of himself as a man.

Getting out, I headed over to the guest house

and knocked.

Hannah's teenage daughter, Kayla, answered the door.

"Hi. My name's Luke. You must be Kayla?"

She nodded but had a shyness about her.

"Is your mother around?"

"Hello," Hannah said, coming up from behind Kayla. "It's almost seven. I thought you'd be here earlier."

"Yeah, sorry about that. I got tied up at work."

"It's all right. Come in." Kayla headed to the second bedroom, which I assumed was the one she took. Meanwhile, Hannah and I took seats on the couch. She had already hung up pictures, set up the television on the entertainment stand, and made the place look like she had been living there for years.

As I surveyed the living room, I turned to her. "Wow. You've been busy. Looks like you've lived here for a while already."

"I don't like living out of boxes."

Raising an eyebrow, I said, "Fair enough. Sorry again about not getting out here sooner. I really meant to."

"Don't worry about it. I understand how life is. Where do you work?"

"*Young's.* I'm an investment banker. But let's not talk about me. I want to know how things are going. Did you get a chance to meet Mac?"

"You mean your dad? Yes." Her lips tightened, and I could sense it wasn't a very pleasant meeting.

"I warned you."

She nodded slowly. "You did warn me. I'll give you that."

Laughing out of nervousness, I said, "He was never the same after he lost my mother to cancer."

"That's sad. I bet he loved her."

"That he did. Did the pastor come out and help?"

"Sure did. He showed up with two dudes who did all the heavy lifting for us. Such a blessing. Do you go to the church out here?"

"Off and on. I live in town, so I mostly attend a church by my house. Charlie's a good man, though. If you're looking for a church family, that's a good one." Glancing toward Kayla's bedroom door, I continued. "Great youth program. They just went to

Mexico not too long ago."

Her countenance fell and her voice quieted. "I don't think Kayla will be attending."

Confused, I asked, "How come?"

Whispering, she leaned toward me, giving me a whiff of the perfume she was wearing, thus only confusing my mind even more than it already was. "She's pregnant."

"Oh, wow."

Leaning back, she seemed to be relaxed after getting it off her chest. Peering over at me, she said, "You know that question in the back of every parent's mind? Wondering if you messed up your children or not? I don't have the question there anymore. I know I botched it."

"You can't blame it on yourself."

"Yeah, I can."

"Care to explain?"

She shook her head. "Do you have kids?"

"No, I don't."

My heart flinched at the question. I knew it was odd to be in my thirties and still have no kids, but there wasn't much I could do about that. I wasn't able to have kids. I had found out this fact from a doctor years ago. I would never know the feeling she mentioned.

"Did you bring the key?" Her voice broke me out of my thoughts.

"Oh, yeah. Sorry." Reaching into my pocket, I pulled out the keychain with three keys on it, along with one of my credit cards. "This one is for the main house, this one the guest house, and then this one is for the shed."

"Shed?"

"Yeah, it's around back of the main house, down the hill by the creek. It doesn't have much in there. Some old gardening equipment of my mother's, and then a snow shovel and the lawn mower. It was on the keyring, so I left it. So for Mac's meals, it's pretty basic. Bacon and eggs for breakfast at seven, a sandwich around noon, and then whatever you can find around the house for dinner. Here's a credit card of mine for groceries. Buy whatever you need for food but keep the receipts."

"Okay. Great." Taking the keys and credit card in her hand, she stood up from the couch.

Taking the cue, I stood up with her. I caught another wonderful whiff of that perfume she was wearing, and I acted without thinking. "I can take you and Kayla around Spokane and show you the city sometime. Maybe grab a bite at the Clinkerdagger, this great restaurant we have."

She shook her head and took a step further away. "Thanks for the offer, Luke, truly, but I think we'll be okay."

I regretted the offer immediately. "Okay."

Kayla walked out into the living room. "Mom. I don't feel so good. Nausea."

Turning her head to Kayla, she said, "Okay. Give me a second."

She walked me to the door. "Thanks again for everything, Luke."

"You're welcome. Take care."

CHAPTER 11-HANNAH

BLINKING MY EYES OPEN THE next morning, it took a full second to realize we weren't still in Flagstaff. The absence of sirens or traffic just outside the window was welcoming. No conversations taking place out on balconies of the residences next door. The silence was not only welcoming, but a pleasant change as I awoke.

Turning my head, I saw it was 6:45am on the alarm clock. I sat up and then got out of bed. Without a care about my appearance, I grabbed the keys off the key hook that Luke had given me and ventured outside the guest house and over to Mac's to start on breakfast.

After making the coffee, I pulled out a frying pan and put it on the stove over medium heat. Grabbing the eggs and bacon from the fridge, I took them over to the stove and set them down. As I did, I caught sight of the salt and pepper shakers. They were the same ones my parents had back when I was a child. Mr. Salt and Mrs. Pepper porcelain characters. I thought about Mac losing his wife and my heart felt a sting of pain for him.

After the eggs were done, I cooked the bacon. As the bacon was frying on the stove, the door that led out to the back opened.

It was Kayla.

With one eye still shut, she sat down at the table and tightened her robe around her frame.

"That smells so good."

Smiling, I flipped the bacon over with the fork. "Grab a plate from the cupboard."

After dishing her up, I took a plate down the hallway in search of Mac's bedroom. Finding the door, I opened it a fraction and saw him sitting up on his bed with his lamp on. He had his nose in a western novel and set it down upon my entering.

He smiled and said, "Thank you," as I set the plate down on his lap.

"Oh, wait. Your bandage."

"I already took care of it. Remember? I don't need help, just food. Could you get me a cup of coffee?"

"Sure. How do you like it?"

"Black."

Grabbing a mugful, I ventured back to his room. Upon entering, I saw that he was finishing a bite.

"So your daughter," he started to say, then wiped his mouth with his napkin. "What's her deal?"

Shaking my head, I shrugged. "What do you mean?"

"I saw her outside by the fence. She was holding a hand against her belly. She pregnant?"

"That's observant of you to notice." I handed him his cup of coffee. "Yes, she is."

"She ought not to treat herself like a used car. She'll end up with too many miles and nobody will want her."

Swallowing my tongue, I flashed a fake smile. "She's sixteen, Mac. She's not a used car. It was one guy." Letting out a sigh as I felt like I had to defend my daughter and my parenting, I continued. "I was not happy about it, trust me. That's why we moved far away from the father."

"Sure. Don't let him be responsible for his own offspring. Sounds about right. Let the government take care of it. Right?"

Furrowing my eyebrows, I said, "Wait one minute. We don't get any assistance from the government, and we won't be starting either. Not that it's any of your business, but she's a good Christian girl and she just made a mistake."

"Christian." He scoffed. "You Christians are pathetic. You ignore the reality all around you and just cling to your crutch of faith like it's going to save you. Tell me where your God is when you're looking into your dying wife's eyes as she fears the ever after. You tell me where he is!" His face was red with anger.

Pausing, I was careful not to say anything.

"What? Be straight with me. I'm straight with you."

"You don't believe in God?"

"No, I know He is real, but that doesn't mean I like Him. He only picks and chooses what He cares about while the rest of us suffer."

"Bad things happen in life, Mac, but it's up to us how we react."

"Nice cliché." Taking a gulp of his coffee, he said, "You'd better keep boys off my property or I'll shoot them. I'm a great shot and I'm not afraid to kill. I'm old. They can lock me up because I'm going to die soon anyway."

"I got to go . . . do anything . . . but this."

Excusing myself quickly from Mac's room, I felt a knot in my chest. He was so pleasant at first when I came in that morning and things took a horrible turn. Returning to the kitchen, I opted to not speak an ill word about Mac to Kayla. I wasn't going to gossip, and that was what it'd be if I spoke a word about the man.

"How's Mac?" she asked, looking up from her eggs.

"He's awake." There. Truthful, yet not gossipy.

Pausing at the counter, I set my hand against the counter as I felt my body weakened from the conversation with Mac. I was going to need God's help to get through the days with this man.

CHAPTER 12-HANNAH

THAT AFTERNOON, I DECIDED TO venture out to the shed to see what was inside. Without a job outside of feeding the grumpy old man and making sure he hadn't fallen every so often, I found myself with more time than I knew what to do with. Walking down the hill and to the old rickety shed, I unfastened the lock using the key Luke had given me.

Opening the doors, the smell of 'old' poured from the darkness. A thick layer of dirt and dust covered the entirety of the shed, only the light from between the boards of the roof shining in. Spotting a wheel barrow and also some basic gardening tools along with a bag of fertilizer, I maneuvered into the shed to retrieve them all. Grabbing the hoe, the gloves, and fertilizer, I loaded them into the wheel barrow.

"Mom?"

I jumped and turned at the sound of Kayla.

"What are you doing?"

"I'm going to work on that garden by the guest house."

She smiled but didn't say anything about the garden. "I tried loading my school's website online and I got an error."

"Did you make sure to use the guest wireless?"

"Yes, Mom. I'm not dumb."

"I'll be there in a second."

She went back up the hill. Shutting and locking

the shed, I pushed the wheel barrow up the hill and parked it in front of the guest house. Wiping the sweat from my forehead, I paused before proceeding inside to help Kayla. I took in a deep breath of the country air. I wasn't sure how Mac could be that angry and bitter living on a property like this, but I knew I needed to focus on the good if I was going to make it through.

Once inside, I walked over to the desk. Kayla moved out of the way and I tried to connect to the wireless network.

Nothing.

Rebooting the computer, I tried again.

Nothing.

"I don't know, dear. I'll shoot a text to Luke and let him know."

"Sweet. No school today. Can we go to town?"

"Newport or Spokane?"

"Newport. I want to see the little town. I was doing research the other day back in Flagstaff online and heard about this really cool statue they have in the middle of town."

"We'll go in a bit. I need seeds to plant anyway. Do you want to help weed the garden?"

She crinkled her nose. "I'm pregnant, Mom. I don't know if that's really good for me to be doing."

I laughed. "You're two months along. You'll be fine! It'll probably even be good for you. Help your mother. Will ya?"

"Okay."

As we ventured outside, Kayla asked about Luke.

"Why'd you turn him down for showing us around Spokane? It was obvious he was interested in you."

"I know, but moving here was about me and you. It's not about finding a guy. We need God and each other. Not Luke."

She stopped. Grabbing my hand, she peered into my eyes. "Mom. I just don't want you to be alone forever, and if it's because of me, worried I'll be hurt, just know I won't be. I am okay with your moving on from dad. Dad was horrible to you, and a new guy might not be. And Luke seemed nice and cute. Just saying."

"Oh, honey . . . no offense to your father, but I learned that things aren't always what they appear to be. Luke was kind to me, yes. He's attractive, yes. But isn't it a little odd that the guy isn't married or in a relationship? Something is off."

"So you'll never date again because of Dad?" She shook her head. "I think you're just scared of falling in love again."

"Don't talk to me that way. You don't know Luke, and neither do I. I can't just throw my heart at any man who shows me the least bit of interest."

She glared at me for a moment as though she was trying to figure me out. "You're not talking about Matt, are you?"

"I said man, not boy."

Raising a hand, she said, "Oh, my goodness, Mother! How dare you! I still love Matt, and I'm sorry I went and messed everything up by getting pregnant!" She started to cry and headed back to the guest house, slamming the door as she went inside.

My heart hemorrhaged with pain. My daughter might have only been sixteen years old, but her words carried the weight of truth when she mentioned my being scared. I was scared, but that was only part of it. I was also unwilling to risk my heart for a man again. Not right now, anyway. Maybe if I knew him more, or maybe down the line, after knowing him a little while longer. And the fact still remained that he was a thirty-something-year-old without a wife or girlfriend, and that was a big, fat red flag.

CHAPTER 13-LUKE

ANSWERING THE PAGE FROM CINDY, I pressed firmly on the button on my phone's speaker system. "Yes?"

"Pamela is on line one. Can I put her through?"

Swallowing hard as my stomach twisted, I paused. Then, I cleared my throat. "No."

Releasing the page, I turned my attention to my computer screen. I was looking up flights to Denver for a meeting next week with a new potential client who was looking to make a major move coming up in August. Amelia ran a pharmaceutical company that dealt mostly in vitamins, and she was looking to buy out a few smaller-sized companies in the Midwest in order to expand her market's reach. If I were able to land this deal, it'd put me over the top for the year and make it the most profitable since I started.

Purchasing the flight, I wheeled around in my chair and stood up. Walking over to the window, I placed my hands in my pockets and looked down at the cars. I thought of Hannah and how she had rejected me the other night. I didn't know what came over me after meeting her, but I immediately felt drawn to her and wanted to see her again in a non-business way. Without an excuse of showing her the town, I'd have to make up some reason to go out there and see my dad.

Another page from Cindy rang through the phone.

I answered in my ear piece.

"You'd better not say Pamela."

"Your brother, Victor, is on line one."

"Patch him through."

"How'd it go with the new tenant?"

"Great. She's already unpacked and settling in. Hopefully, she isn't scared off by Dad."

"He's a hard guy to be around, but he has a lot of wisdom tucked in between the hard edges. I'm sure she'll be fine. That last gal was just a flake."

I rubbed my brow as I turned away from the window and approached my desk. "I goofed up and asked her out."

"Oh, jeez, Luke. Why? You don't go out with anyone. Why this girl?"

"I don't know. She seemed different. I think I might go out there and apologize for asking her out."

"No, man. Don't do that. She'll think you're a freak if you go out there and just apologize."

"Well, I need to go see Dad anyway."

He laughed. "No, you don't. Just stay away from her or she'll really run away. Imagine if you hit on an employee at your work? That'd be horrible for the gal. She's basically your employee in the situation with Dad."

"I hadn't thought of it like that. Man, I'm an idiot. Wait, I have to go out there."

"What? Why?"

"Dad's monthly prescription is at the pharmacy and I have to take it out to him. He's about out."

"Ahh. There you go. You have a reason to see her

again, I guess. But please try to leave the poor gal alone. She's been through enough with moving."

"Stop acting like you don't know me. You know it wasn't like me to ask her out like that to begin with."

"I know it's unlike you. That's what worries me. I haven't heard you this joyous in a while. Plus, we both know you *love* the knight in shining armor scenario where you can swoop in and save the day. Pamela—"

"Don't go there, Victor."

After hanging up with my brother, I continued to work through the day. The day's work felt slow and sluggish, though, as I anticipated seeing Hannah again. I couldn't stop thinking about those gorgeous soft eyes and the smell of her perfume.

CHAPTER 14-HANNAH

MY BACK ACHED AND SWEAT poured from my forehead as I finally finished my day's work in the garden. The worn metal garbage can I found behind the guest house sat full to the brim with the weeds I had pulled. Along with weeding, I had tilled the dirt and mixed in fertilizer to help revitalize the soil. It felt good to get my hands dirty, to labor in the warmth of the sun.

Taking off my gardening gloves, I tossed them into the wheel barrow along with the empty fertilizer bag. Breathing deeply as I pushed it back toward the hill that led to the shed, I recalled my greenhouse. It was a tranquil place for me, a place where I felt the presence of God as I was surrounded by His creation all around me. It was my favorite place to pray.

As I came over the slope of the hill, I spotted a black bear in the shallows of the creek.

I jolted to a stop. My heart racing, my steps were frozen.

The bear was monstrous in size, easily over two hundred pounds. Thankfully, the bear's back was toward me and I was able to gently set the wheel barrow down. Carefully, I backed my steps up.

With the bear out of my sight, I turned and sprinted to Mac's house. Placing my trembling hand on the doorknob, I let myself in.

"Mac?" I called for him, my words shaky, trembling.

"In my room," he replied.

Hurrying my way down the hall, I could feel my heartbeat in my ears. Arriving in the doorway, I said, "There's a bear down in the creek."

He moved his legs over the side of the bed and grabbed for his crutches that were leaned against his nightstand. Grabbing them, he turned to me. "Grab my rifle from under the bed."

Hurriedly, I got down on my knees and reached my trembling hand underneath. My fingers found the gun. Pulling it out, I stood up just as he was up and coming around the end of the bed.

"We haven't much time." He maneuvered past me, leading the way.

We came to the top of the hill and looked down.

The bear was gone.

"I swear it was there!"

He nodded. "I know. It was Betsy. Black bears aren't seen a whole lot in these parts, but I know of at least one—Betsy. She likes the fish in this creek."

"Really? Luke didn't tell me about bears being out here!"

"This ain't Arizona, kid. You think bears are scary? Wait until you see a cougar. Those are the real killers." His eyes drifted to the wheel barrow. "What were you doing with the wheel barrow?"

My pulse was calming. Turning around, I pointed toward the garden. "I'm working on the garden. It looks like someone used to keep up with it."

His expression hardened. "Who told you that you could do that?"

An uncomfortable feeling settled over me. This wasn't a guy you wanted to upset. "Um. I had a key to the shed and I figured it wouldn't be a big deal. I'm sorry if you didn't want me to do that."

"Next time, ask if you're going to be digging around my property."

"Want me to re-plant the weeds and remove the fertilizer?"

His hardened face softened, and he laughed. "You do have a sense of humor. Listen, just make sure you don't plant any berries. Betsy loves her berries."

"All right."

"You can hold onto that gun. Keep yourself safe."

"Thanks."

Just then, Kayla came around the corner from the guest house and over to us.

"What's going on? Why are you holding a gun, Mom?"

"Protection."

She raised an eyebrow. "Why?"

"We're living in bear country now, dear. Come on, let's go get ready and go into town."

Mac stayed put as I ventured back to the guest house with Kayla. Glancing over my shoulder as we walked, I didn't just see a grumpy old man anymore. I saw a person who had a past with a bear named Betsy. But not just with the bear. I suspected his wife had something to do with that garden and his reaction over it. There was more to that man than just the hard front he showed people. As Kayla and I

91

went inside, I lifted a prayer up for Mac. Only God

would know how to break through to him.

CHAPTER 15-LUKE

IT WAS ALREADY A QUARTER past six o'clock when I finally got out of the office in Spokane. I planned to leave at three, but what I planned never seemed to match reality. Getting over to the pharmacy on Francis for my father, I had my excuse now in hand to see her again. On my drive out, I tried to piece together an apology for the forwardness I had exhibited the other night, but I came up short on what to say.

Along the interstate, I caught sight of a woman and child on the side of the road. They were standing in front of their van with the hood propped open.

Moved with compassion, I pulled over.

"What seems to be the problem, miss?" I asked,

approaching them as I tried not to get run over by the passing cars.

She shrugged. "I don't know. The *Check Engine* light came on and then it just started smoking, so I pulled over."

My phone rang.

Slipping my cell phone out from my pocket, I saw it was Pamela and hit *Ignore*.

"Sorry. Let's have a look."

Glancing under the hood, I attempted to figure out the issue. Pausing, I turned to her as she stood by. "Was it white smoke?"

"Yes. Then it stopped once I pulled over and shut the van off for a bit."

"How long ago was that?"

"I don't know. About a half hour or so. I called my brother, and he's supposed to be coming out, but I don't know when. He's going to call me back."

"Okay." Taking off my button-up shirt but leaving my undershirt on, I turned to the lady once again. "You and your son should stand back. I'm not sure if it's still hot."

They took a step back from the van.

Keeping my head cocked back to protect my eyes, I opened the coolant cap.

Nothing. I breathed a sigh of relief.

Glancing inside, I saw it was low.

"I think you're low on coolant. Possible crack or leak somewhere. Do you have some water?"

"I have a water tumbler. Would that help?"

"Yes."

She went to get it out of the front seat, leaving the boy nearby. Glancing down at the blond-haired, blue-eyed child who was probably about eight, I remembered the day I found out I couldn't have children. Pamela and I had been trying at that point for two long years. I sat in a waiting room at the hospital in a hard plastic chair as I waited for the results. Pamela had an appointment on that day, so I was waiting alone. Then, they called me up to the window. I remember walking away from the nurse at the window with a deafening sound in my ears that rang clear into my soul. I thought God hated me for a long time. Pamela had wanted children. This little blond boy looked similar to the little boy I'd imagined we'd have with my blue eyes and her blonde hair.

Snapping back to reality, I asked the kid, "How are you?"

He took a step back and furrowed his eyebrows.

I laughed a little. "Smart boy. You shouldn't talk to strangers."

Coming back only a moment later, the lady handed me a turquoise tumbler that was half-full of water. "More water would be ideal, but this should at least get you up the road to a mechanic."

Dumping the contents in, I returned the cap and shut the hood.

"Thank you so much for the help."

Wiping my hands off on the now dirty button-up shirt, I said, "You're welcome."

"Can you tell me where a mechanic is up the

road?"

"Sure. It's in Newport. Nice little town, just up a few miles. Mikey's Mechanic Shop is where you'll end up. Tell them Mac's son Luke sent you."

"Thanks again for the help, Luke."

"No problem. Cute kid. Take care."

Returning to my car, I waited to make sure she was able to start the van back up and pull onto the freeway. As I waited, I thought of the missed call from Pamela. Avoiding her forever wasn't an option, and soon, I'd have to face the reality that was before me that involved the two of us. Time had run its course.

CHAPTER 16-HANNAH

AFTER PICKING UP A FEW types of seeds at the hardware store in Newport, Kayla and I parked on the side of the road in downtown Newport to go see the bell statue that she had read about. It was smack dab in the middle of town and looked to hold a significance to the residents and history of Newport.

Getting out of the car, I looked over at Kayla.

"Looks to be in great condition."

"Yeah. According to what I read, the bell had been lost in Diamond Lake when it was on a boat. They found it a few years ago and pulled it out. They keep cameras on it so nobody steals it." She laughed, then her gaze turned to the town's buildings and shops that lined the streets. "This town is so cute.

I've always read about these kinds of places, but I've never seen one before."

"And it's our new home. How fun is that?" She smiled, and I joined her side. We crossed the street to the island in the middle of the road that held the statue.

"It's hard to imagine this is where we live now." Her hand grazed her belly as her countenance fell. "I miss Matt, mom. I'm homesick."

"You'll get used to it. Promise."

As we walked up to the statue, she said, "He's going to visit next month."

"What?" My tone was defensive, my anger boiling.

"Matthew. He's going to visit and bring clothes

for the baby. He said we're going to make it work even if it's long-distance."

"He can't stay with us."

"How come?" she asked, taking a step back as I saw tears well in her eyes.

"Because I said so. Plus, I'm pretty sure Mac might kill him."

"Fine. He'll stay in Newport."

"Dear . . ."

"I'm an adult, mother. You can't just baby me forever."

"When you turn eighteen, you can go make your own dumb decisions, but until then, I'm the mom!"

She was quiet, her gaze elsewhere and her face

twisted.

We walked silently back across the street to the car. Seeing a thrift store on the side of the road we were parked on, I pointed to it. "We still need a crib. Maybe we can check in there?"

Before she said anything, Pastor Charlie and a woman I assumed was his wife came walking out of the thrift store.

"Hey, Hannah," Charlie said. Turning to the woman, he said, "Serenah. This is the lady and her daughter I told you about last night."

"Nice to put a face to the name. I'm Serenah." She reached out a hand to greet me.

"Nice to meet you. This is my daughter, Kayla."

They shook hands.

"Thanks for loaning your hubby out for the afternoon yesterday."

Smiling, she waved her hand through the air. "No problem. He loves that kind of work."

"Mom. I'm going to go in and look around," Kayla said, obviously annoyed with our conversation and motioning with her head toward the thrift store.

"Okay."

She headed through the doorway into the thrift shop. I could tell the two of them noticed her bad attitude, so I apologized.

"Sorry about that. She's still adjusting."

Serenah turned to Charlie. "Go ahead and head to the diner. I'll catch up with you in a few."

He kissed her cheek and left.

Leading me over to a nearby bench, Serenah motioned for me to join her. We sat down. Glancing over her shoulder at the thrift store, she said, "Being sixteen is hard."

"Yeah, especially sixteen and pregnant."

Her eyes went wide. "She's pregnant?"

"Oh. I thought Charlie would've told you."

Shaking her head, she said, "No. He didn't, and he wouldn't. He tries to keep people's lives private. Otherwise, it could be construed as gossip."

"I don't know what to do with her. She's so up and down, left and right."

She nodded slowly but didn't say anything.

"You're a pastor's wife. Could you give me advice?"

"I'll say this. She's going to struggle for a while with just being sixteen and moving here. Toss in being pregnant, and she's bound to be an emotional wreck. Just remember that the more you try to control, the more you lose the control. Let her fall down, skin her knees, get dirty, be sad."

"I'm sorry to put you on the spot and dump this on you."

Serenah shook her head. "It's fine. I remember when I first moved here. It was hard. I was pregnant and scared. Keep trusting God, Hannah. You can't go wrong with God."

Smiling, I nodded. "You seem so perfect. Like this angel that just shows up on the sidewalk and speaks truth and wisdom."

Shaking her head as her chin dipped, she giggled

a little. "I'm no angel, and I've been through my fair share of struggles. Whatever you think you might see that is good in me is only God. We're all fallen and messed up. Sometimes, you know a person's struggle and sometimes, you don't."

"Mom." Kayla's voice radiated from behind me. Turning, I saw her standing with the thrift store door wide open. "There's a really cute crib in here. Come look."

"Just a minute, dear. I'll be right there!"

"I don't mean to hold you up. I have to get going over to the diner anyway."

We stood up.

"Thank you, and it was truly a blessing to meet you, Serenah."

Parting ways, I couldn't help but feel like God had brought her into my life at that very moment to nudge me in a different direction with Kayla and Matt. I knew now that if I made Kayla angry and tried to break them up, she'd be even more obsessed with making it work. There had to be a point in which I let loose of the control and let God be God. If it was God's will for them to break up, it'd happen.

CHAPTER 17-LUKE

DISPLEASED TO SEE HANNAH'S CAR missing

from the driveway, I had half a notion to leave, but I

did need to drop off my dad's prescription. Parking

outside the main house, I glanced over at the guest

house on my way up the porch. Giving a light knock,

I let myself in.

Walking in, I ventured down the hallway and to

his bedroom. Taking a deep breath, I grabbed hold

of the doorknob and went in.

He was asleep. I was thankful for this fact.

I moved with carefulness not to wake him and

made my way to his closet. I grabbed one of my

dress shirts I had left there a while ago. Then I

moved to the side of the bed and set the bag of

medicine down on the night stand. Turning around,

I started for the door when he said, "Thanks, sonny boy."

Turning around, I said, "I thought you were sleeping."

He propped himself up on the bed and shook his head, but he looked to be dwelling on something. "I wasn't asleep. Just resting my eyes."

"What's up? You seem distracted."

"Betsy's back."

Raising my eyebrow as I thought about the black bear that had caused so much trouble for him several years ago, I came over to the bed and sat down. He'd named the bear Betsy after his older sister, and it was just as mean and cruel as the real person it had been named after. Betsy and Dad were placed in a foster home at the ages of six and eight.

She'd always told him he had to be tough if he wanted to make it in the real world and thought that constantly beating him up would do just that. Before she died a few years back, she found my father passed out drunk in the front yard after he lost my mom and thought it'd be a good idea to pour maple syrup all over his back and coat him in tuna fish. He woke up to a black bear swiping his flesh from his back like a fork shredding chicken. He was left with scars on his back, but he never touched the bottle again after that. My dad never called the police, even though I recommended he should.

"What are you going to do?"

"I'll tell you what I'm going to do, sonny boy. I'm going to kill her."

"It's just a bear, Dad. Do you really need to kill

the thing?"

He nodded confidently as he stared blankly toward the window. "I need my revenge."

"Okay. Hey, where's Hannah?"

"She said she was running into town for some stuff. Did you know she is working on your mother's garden?"

"I didn't notice."

"She seems to be getting cozy quickly around here."

"Are you actually liking her around?" Shock coursed through me. I had expected a battle to have her stay.

"She's all right. I'm more worried about the kid. She doesn't have a dad and she's pregnant. No man in her life."

"What about you? You're a man."

He paused and looked surprised.

"What? I thought you resented me for the way I raised you."

Shaking my head, I walked over to the window as I saw Hannah pulling into the driveway. "I don't resent you, Dad. I just didn't have a good example of how to be a man when I grew up. This is a second chance for you to do it right. I'm not telling you what to do. Just think about it."

"That's an interesting notion."

"I'm going to go see if Hannah needs help with anything."

Leaving my dad's bedroom, I headed outside to

greet Hannah and Kayla.

CHAPTER 18-HANNAH

PULLING OUT THE CRIB IN pieces, I set them against the back of my car and shut the trunk. As Kayla and I picked up sides of the crib, Luke came out of Mac's house and jogged over to us in the driveway. He had a white dress shirt on, a few buttons undone on top, and a pair of blue jeans on. He carried the scent of oil mixed with cologne and reminded me of a different time in my life. Growing up, my parents were poor, and my father was always outside working on something to do with our car. He'd come in for dinner and always carry the smell of oil.

"Need a hand?" Luke offered.

I shook my head, but Kayla wasn't shy.

"Yes, we do! The guy at the thrift store had to

break it down into pieces, and last summer, we couldn't even build a simple book case! Your being here is a divine appointment. Right, Mom?"

"Right."

Smiling, he glanced over at me. "I can help. If you'll have me."

I shrugged. "Sure."

He grabbed all the rest of the pieces at the back of the car, and we all ventured toward the guest house. His eyes caught sight of my garden. "What are you planting?"

"Peas, maybe some carrots. Nothing much."

"Cool. Back in the day, my mother had a strawberry patch there. I helped her with canning the best jam in the world."

"That's really cool. I don't believe I've ever had homemade jam before," Kayla chimed in.

Getting inside the guest house, I was relieved to feel the coolness of the ceiling fan in the living room. We set all the pieces down in the living room for Luke to assemble. Kayla went to her room to organize it and make a spot for where the crib could go.

"It's a bit early for a crib, but for only ten bucks, we couldn't pass it up."

"That's a great deal."

Half an hour later, Luke had worked up a good sweat building the crib, so I brought him a glass of water. Pausing, he stood up and took a long drink. Setting the cup down on the coffee table, he looked over at me. "Sorry about the other day. I shouldn't have been so forward."

"Don't be sorry. I'm just wary of guys since my divorce."

"I bet, and I understand."

He paused, glancing at the floor for a second. Then he shook his head, his eyes lifting to mine. "I'm really sorry that happened to you."

"It's okay."

"No. It absolutely is not okay."

He pieced together most of the crib, moved the pieces into Kayla's room, and then finished putting it together. Once done, he cleaned up his tools. On his way to the front door to leave, he saw Mac's rifle sitting against the wall. He pointed to the gun. "You have my dad's gun?"

"Yeah. He wants me to protect myself, but I don't know where to begin."

"Not leaving a gun lying around would be a good start." Grabbing the gun, he checked to see if the safety was on. He handed the gun to me. "I can teach you to shoot."

I nodded. "I'd like that."

"I'll come by this weekend. On Saturday around one? If that works for you?"

"All right. Thanks again for putting the crib together. We would've struggled to get it together before the baby comes in seven months."

He laughed. "You're welcome. Take care."

Luke left out the front door, and I watched as he went out to his car. Kayla came up beside me and rested her head against my shoulder.

"He seems like a really good guy, Mom."

"I know."

Turning to me, she said, "I just got off the phone with Matt. He bought his bus ticket for next month. I told him about staying in a hotel while he is here, and he was upset, but he understood. You sure you're not going to freak out that he's in Newport?"

Of course I was upset he was going to be in Newport, but I didn't want to add fuel to the growing and ever-burning desire she had to be with Matt. I knew, after speaking with Serenah, that I needed to take a step backward. Yes, he had gotten my sixteen-year-old pregnant, and yes, I did move away from Flagstaff to create a new start for us. But God was ultimately the One in control, and I had to place my trust in Him.

"I have no problem with that. I have to go make Mac and us dinner. I'll be back in a bit."

Walking over to Mac's house, I saw the taillights of Luke's car vanish up into the thicket of trees surrounding the driveway, and my heart rate picked up its pace. I realized just then that I looked forward to seeing him in two days.

CHAPTER 19-HANNAH

THAT EVENING, DINNER WAS DELIGHTFUL for Mac, myself, and Kayla. Mac hadn't said one ill word through the entirety of the meal at the kitchen table. I was thankful he had put his brash way of speaking on the back burner while Kayla was around. It was one thing to be rough in the way he spoke to me, another adult, but to my daughter, who was already on edge from moment to moment, was an entirely different thing.

Clearing her plate from the table while I started on dishes, Kayla came closer to my side. "I'm going to go sit at the picnic table out back and watch the sunset."

"Okay."

"Mind if I join you?" Mac asked, catching the

both of us off guard.

Kayla and I looked at each other for a second. I shrugged.

"Sure," she said respectfully.

I continued washing dishes and started praising God in my heart.

Mac grabbed his crutches and they went out the back door together. Mac might have been a little rough around the edges, but I was suspecting there was some good buried in there after all. After rinsing the dishes and setting them in the dish drain, I ventured over to the open window and leaned against the wall out of sight. I wanted to listen in on the two of them.

"I agree, but you can't let your mistakes define you, kid." Mac's words carried a weight of absolution to them. Glancing out the window, I saw that Kayla's chin dipped. She looked sad. I began to wonder what he was telling my daughter.

"But I made my mom so upset. I know she hates Matt for it, and that's why we moved out here. She wants us to break up, but I won't allow it."

"Maybe she does, but she is your mom. She cares about you."

"Yeah." Kayla's response was with an air of sarcasm.

"Hey, now. She does. You know she does."

"I know . . ." Kayla said, her tone respectful, reserved. For a second, I felt overwhelmed with jealousy at how calm she was remaining with Mac. Part of me wanted to run out there and ask her why she couldn't ever listen to me the way she was

123

listening to him, but I didn't. I stayed quiet and listened on.

"You might have a little one on the way, kid, but that doesn't mean your life is over. It just means you have to grow up quicker than by design."

"Design? Like by God?"

Mac went quiet. I suspected the 'design' comment had slipped out without his meaning to. Then, he turned to her. "Yeah. God's design. But he's a good God, and while you make plans, He will help you take the steps. Everything will work out in the end, and if it doesn't, it's not over yet."

Confusion swirled my thoughts as I recalled his harsh words against God the other day to me. When I heard them getting up from the picnic table, I hurried my steps away from the window in the kitchen and grabbed a plate from the dish drain.

They came back inside, and I set the plate into the dish drain as I turned to them.

Mac headed down the hallway to his bedroom while Kayla came over to me.

"You have a good talk with Mac?"

"Yeah, he's cool."

We began walking out of the kitchen to go through the living room and out the front door. I stopped and turned to Kayla as we reached the door. "You go ahead. I need to talk to Mac for a second."

"What? Why? He was nice, Mom. I promise."

"I understand. It's not about him talking to you."

"Okay."

Kayla left out the door, and I went down the hallway in pursuit of Mac. I wanted to confront him about the comments he made about God. It was more out of curiosity than anything else.

Knocking lightly on his bedroom door, I walked in without waiting for a reply.

His shirt was off and his back was to me.

My insides tensed as my gaze fell upon his scarred back.

Large and painful grooves were carved into his skin like filleted pieces of meat.

"Sorry!" I offered quickly and stepped back, shutting the door as my heart sank.

"It's fine, come in."

Opening the door again, I was apprehensive but

relieved to see he had a shirt on now.

I didn't say anything as I walked in.

"What is it you need, Hannah?"

"Sorry. I just wanted to ask you something, but I feel stupid now."

"Well, it'd be dumb if you left without asking it now. Speak your peace."

"Well . . ." I took a few more steps over to the bed. "I overheard part of your conversation with Kayla."

Raising a hand, he said, "I'm sorry if I overstepped my bounds, but that girl needed to hear it."

"No, I wasn't upset about anything you said. Just curious. Why'd you mention God?"

He went quiet, his gaze turning to the window in his room for a few moments. Then he looked back at me. "I never said I don't believe in God. In fact, I did mention that I do believe in Him, if I recall." Folding his hands on his lap, he looked down at his thumbs as he twirled them over top of one another. "My late wife made me a better person, and when I was talking to your daughter, I thought about her. Thought about what she'd want me to say. The thought that came to my mind was 'give the girl hope.' You see, I might be angry about God taking my sweet wife away from me, but I know the importance of hope for someone. Hope for the future."

"Do you have hope?" I asked without thinking. When he didn't respond right away, I apologized. "Sorry."

"No, don't be. It's a good question. I have hope to see my wife again someday in heaven. I also have hope to see Jesus, even if I didn't like how things in my life turned out."

All this talk of Jesus and God made me wonder why he was the way that he was.

"I know what you're thinking. You want to know why I'm bitter. You know why? Because I lost a part of me when God took her. He took her away and I wasn't ready! The day I lost Rita, I lost a part of myself I'll never back. All that's left is this grumpy shell of a man I used to be."

"I couldn't imagine . . ."

Glancing at his watch, he said, "Yeah, well, anyway. *Gunsmoke* is about to be on."

"All right. Thank you for talking to her. Have a

good night."

"Don't mention it. You two have a good night as well."

Leaving Mac's shortly thereafter, I knew God brought me to his ranch for a reason and it had to do with Mac. My love for God, even after all the pain I had been through with Jonathan, hadn't changed. Though I didn't lose Jonathan through a sudden death, I felt our pains were similar. My world, too, had crumbled all around me, just as it had for Mac. Prompted in my heart, I knew that God wanted me to share my faith with Mac. I just wasn't sure how I could do that yet.

CHAPTER 20-LUKE

MEETING WITH THE MEDIATOR ON Friday morning, I hoped to end this matter once and for all with Pamela. I hadn't called her back but instead elected to act on my own for what I knew she wanted from me. I phoned the mediator yesterday and set up the appointment myself. Wearing the nicest suit in my closet, I walked in *Benson's Law Office* and met with Herbert Ashenburger, the one who had been facilitating our divorce.

Pouring myself a glass of ice water from the pitcher in the board room, I took a large drink from my glass and set it on the table. I didn't like waiting. Rubbing the corner of the glass with my thumb, I thought over the last year and a half and the ongoing battle between my lawyers and Pamela's. It was ugly, it was brutal, and it was ruthless. For a marriage that only lasted a couple of years, it had been dragged out far too long and it needed to end.

"Sorry about the wait." Herbert came into the board room and shut the door behind him. He sat down in the leather swivel chair in front of me and set the file down on the table. That manila folder held more than just some papers. It held the demands my soon to be ex-wife was insisting on in order to grant me the final divorce, the unreasonable request to give up the house I bought, the Lexus she couldn't live without, and a generous alimony to keep up with her lavish lifestyle.

"I'm ready to negotiate."

"What? She has to be here if you came in to *negotiate*, Luke."

"I mean, I'm ready to sign it all away."

Taking off his glasses, he set them down on the table and leaned back in his chair. Lifting a leg up, he crossed it over his other one as he relaxed. "Really? After all this time, you're just going to give it up?"

"I'm done with it. I'm done seeing her, hearing from her. I just want it over, once and for all."

"Even the alimony and the house?"

"She already lives there. She can have it. The alimony is fine as long as it is removed in the event she gets married."

"Great." Sitting up in his chair, he opened the file and started handing over the papers to sign. With each paper I signed, I felt one step closer to freedom from Pamela's phone calls and pestering. With the freedom came a certain deep abiding sorrow in my soul. The end of a marriage ordained by God was nothing to be happy about, even when the presence of sin was found to be true. There was no changing Pamela's mind about the divorce. God knows how long I tried.

Meeting Hannah and feeling an attraction toward her might have spurred me to action on the matter, but it was my heart's way of telling me to move on. It wasn't she who brought me in to see Herbert. It was God, and I knew it. God had shown me that it was time to put the past to rest and let go of the material items I was trying to cling to. God didn't care about the Lexus or any of the money I had in the bank. He cared about my heart. I hoped Hannah was in that plan He had for my life, but I knew that could never be even a remote possibility as long as I was married.

Signing the last document, I set the pen down with a feeling of absolution.

Pamela had cheated on me and ripped my heart out by becoming pregnant with my best friend's child. Along with my heart, she took my house, my car, and my money.

While I looked forward to the future and what God had in store for me, it wasn't without a bit of apprehensiveness. When I shared with Pamela that I couldn't ever give her children, she went out and found someone who could.

CHAPTER 21-HANNAH

SATURDAY AFTERNOON, I WAS A hot mess while
I awaited the highly anticipated arrival of Luke on
the ranch. I spent far too long in front of the mirror
trying to get my hair into the perfect look and ended
up making it look ridiculous. Mac was also on my
mind. Our conversation the other evening about
God and the pain of his losing his wife weighed
heavily on my heart and was in my prayers since I'd
heard it. We hadn't spoken about the matter since
that night, but I kept thinking about how I could
share my own faith. Then it came to me early that
morning during my devotional time with God. I was
reading in the book of James in the Bible.

Come near to God and he will come near to you.
Wash your hands, you sinners, and purify your

hearts, you double-minded.

James 4:8

The verse brought me a sense of clarity over the matter with Mac and God, and with myself and Jonathan. While I drew closer to God when the unexpected happened, Mac withdrew. As I came closer to God, God came closer to me. Now, if only I could figure out a way to share that with Mac. There was the option of going right up to him and showing him the Scripture, but I wasn't sure that would work well.

The doorbell rang, and I exited the bathroom to go answer it.

Upon opening the door, I was surprised at how he was dressed but pleased with the look. While I'd spent way too much time on my hair and outfit,

Luke looked like he had just rolled out of bed and put a pair of jeans and a white V-neck on. His hair was messy, and he didn't appear to have shaved either. But he pulled it off marvelously, like it was all on purpose.

"Luke."

He took his shades off.

"Hannah." He opened the screen door and I let him inside. Stepping in, he looked me in the eyes. "You think you're ready for this?"

Laughing as I thought he was talking about himself, I said, "What?"

He reached over to the gun and picked it up. "To shoot?"

"Oh. Yeah. For sure."

"Good. Let's go out the back. There's a target over in the woods not far from here."

He led the way and I followed. As we walked outside and I shut the door behind me, I thought of Mac again. What better person to ask than his own son? "Do you think if I showed your dad a Bible passage, he'd get upset?"

He stopped and turned around.

"Why would you do that?" He took a defensive tone and stance as his eyebrows furrowed.

"Well, we were talking about God the other night."

"Honestly, I'd save your breath talking about God with Mac. He's not the type of guy who takes too kindly to advice. Especially when it comes to God. As much as I would love my dad to love God

139

again, I really need y'all to work out in this caretaker position. With that being said, it's best not to rock the boat."

Luke continued toward the woods, and I followed.

Stepping over a rotted log, I continued. "But he was talking to Kayla about God and giving her hope."

He stopped again. He lifted an eyebrow as he turned to me. "Really?"

"Yes. That's why I feel like he might really like what I figured out this morning. It's Scripture, and he believes in God."

"You can try to share it with him, but chances aren't good he'll hear you. Everybody can hear the words of the Bible, but only a few can and will 'do' what it says."

"Noted. Thanks." Inquiring with Luke about his father was about as effective as asking one of these rocks out on the forest's floor—not helpful. I did learn something about Mac from Luke though. I learned that he was surprised to hear of his father speaking in a positive way about God. I suspected God was up to something in Mac, and it not only involved my coming out here, but it very well could involve Kayla too.

CHAPTER 22-LUKE

FINALLY FINDING THE OLD CUSHION in the woods my brother and I used for a target years ago, I bent at the knees and brushed off the leaves and other debris. Lifting the cushion up, I set it against a nearby tree and took a step back as I surveyed its condition. It was well-aged and a memento from my past growing up out here on the ranch with Victor. We'd always come out into the woods and shoot our guns every weekend. It didn't matter if there was sunshine or two feet of snow on the ground. We always shot, and we always did it together.

Backpedaling my steps to where Hannah was standing yards away from the target, I handed her the gun.

She held it up, the stock under her arm, not

pressed against her shoulder.

"Whoa. Wait." Stepping up to her, I lifted the gun in her hands and positioned the stock against the front part of her shoulder. "You want it here."

Being that close to Hannah gave me a whiff of her perfume. Some sort of melon, fruity smell invaded my nostrils. The perfume mingled with her scent and created an intoxicating smell that made it hard to concentrate.

I stepped back.

"Like this?" she asked, glancing over at me as she appeared nervous holding the gun.

"Yes. Now aim down the sight and take the safety off. Then, place your finger on the trigger."

She did.

"Okay. Now shoot."

A long minute passed, then she fired.

"Safety back on."

She put the safety back on, then pointed the gun to the ground. I traveled the forest floor to the target. To my surprise, she had not only hit the target but came fairly close to the center ring. Turning back to her, I flashed her a thumbs-up. "Great first shot! You came pretty close to the bull's-eye."

She shrugged and smiled, trying to play it off like it was no big deal. "I guess I'm just a natural shot, Luke."

"Beginner's luck!" I said with a smile.

After we practiced shooting for a while, we were

about to head back to the guest house when I noticed a familiar trail in the woods. "You want to go for a walk? There's an old trail over here my brother and I always went on."

"I'd like that."

As we walked in the shade of the towering trees, I stole glances of Hannah as she took in her surroundings.

"This place is beautiful, isn't it?" My question came as we journeyed down a slope. She didn't know it, but we were coming up quick on the creek that ran through the property. I wanted to show her my 'thinking rock'.

"It really is," she replied as she stepped over a downed tree.

We pushed through a thick patch of shrubs and

forestry overgrowth and finally arrived at the water. The soft sound of the water gliding over rocks cultivated a familiar easygoing feeling within me that reminded me of my visits to this same spot as a child.

Pointing out a large boulder that was lodged in the creek about a foot in, I glanced at her. "That's the spot I used to come to as a child. I'd sit there for hours and just listen to the creek as I read."

Smiling, she passed by me and jumped out to the rock. Laughing as she landed in a crouched position, she sat down. Peering at me, she scooted over to one side and raised an eyebrow. "You coming?"

I smiled and made my way out to the boulder.

Sitting down beside her, I took in the beauty of

the forest and the beauty of the woman sitting beside me. I never thought in a million years that I'd be sitting on this rock with a girl some twenty years later.

Kicking off her shoes, she dipped her toes in. "I bet it was amazing to grow up out here."

"It had good parts and bad parts. The bus ride to school was forever long."

Letting out a surprised bark of laughter, she grinned at me. "Ahh . . . yeah. I bet that part was annoying." Her eyes lifted and surveyed the trees and their leaves blocking out part of the sky above our heads. "But there is so much of God's beauty out here. The mountains, the trees, the creek."

"I like the way you see the world."

My words brought a smile to her face.

Later that afternoon, we walked back to the guest house. I felt a certain bond with her now that we had spent time together most of the afternoon. I didn't want our time to end and I had a feeling she didn't either. Stopping just short of the door, I asked, "Want to go into town and grab some dinner?"

"I can't."

Immediately, I regretted asking. "I'm sorry. I shouldn't have asked. You already said 'no' to me the other day. I thought—"

She grabbed my arm. "No, it's not that I don't want to. I have to cook for Mac or I would."

"I'll cook for him!" Kayla said from the kitchen window of the guest house. We had no idea she was standing there listening to our conversation, but I was glad to hear her offer up the help.

Raising an eyebrow as I peered over at Hannah, I waited for her response. I didn't want to push anymore. It was up to her.

"Great! Let me change and grab my purse and we can go."

Hannah and I headed into the house. She headed to her bedroom to change and Kayla came into the living room.

"Please don't hurt my mom."

Caught off guard, I shook my head. "I wouldn't dream of it. You don't have to worry about that. I can assure you."

Her gaze fell to her mother's door, then back to me. "She's done a lot for me and I love her so much.

I want her to be happy, and I really think she could be with you."

Not if she wants more kids, I thought to myself. Trying to shove my insecurities away, I shrugged. "That's sweet of you, but you don't even know me."

"That is true." She nodded. "But I have to believe that God brought my mom and me out here for a reason. I have to have hope not only for me, but for my mom to be able to find happiness."

"Not everything in God's plan results in sunshine and rainbows. Paul, who wrote most of the New Testament, was brutally killed."

Her eyes widened.

Raising a hand, I said, "Sorry."

"It's okay. I know your father."

The bedroom door opened a moment later, and Hannah came out. She had ditched her jeans for a black skirt and a blue cardigan and white blouse.

"Wow. You did all of this in a couple of minutes?"

She blushed. "I wanted to be cute on our date and I knew you were waiting."

Warmth radiated through my heart as I heard her say the word *date.* I immediately prayed and asked God to direct me moving forward and to help me reveal to Hannah the truth about Pamela, the truth about never being able to have kids.

CHAPTER 23-HANNAH

AS WE FINISHED OUR MEALS, LUKE WIPED his mouth with his napkin. Then, he took a drink from his glass of ice water. "I have a meeting with a potential client next week in Colorado."

My heart slammed on the brakes, refusing to continue the tumble into liking him more. Suddenly, I was back to my first marriage with Jonathan, him sitting across from me back in Phoenix and explaining how he'd be traveling to Florida for business. I tried my best to fight the temptation to equate Luke to my ex-husband, but my strength failed. My pulse began to race and I became increasingly troubled.

"Oh, yeah?" It was a futile attempt to keep the dialog going, but I was more focused on trying to calm my insecurities inside that were surfacing with a vengeance. I thought I had been healed from the pains of my past, but they had come to the forefront of my mind. Why would God put a man in my life who would only remind me of the painful past? My insides twisted with uneasiness. Reaching for my glass of water, I took a drink.

"She's running this awesome tech company that is just now starting to expand and grow. I think I can really help her."

I choked on my water and set the glass down quickly, grabbing the napkin to wipe my lips. Not only was he traveling out of town, but his client was a woman. My chest tightened as my insecurities only seemed to flare with each new piece of information. Already outside the restaurant and hailing a cab, my heart had left the table.

153

"Something wrong?" He placed a hand on the table, leaning across it slightly as he stared at me.

"No. Sorry," I lied. Then I went ahead and lied again to save face. "Um. I just was thinking about Kayla. She's been having heartburn a lot lately, and I need to get her some *Zantac* on the way home."

"Oh. Okay. We'll grab some for her on the way back to the ranch. You know what works surprisingly well? Apple cider vinegar. Two teaspoons in a glass of water cures it every time for me. I used to suffer from it a lot years ago."

"I'll have to try that."

He must've sensed I didn't like our conversation pertaining to his job and client, because the next thing out of his mouth had nothing to do with it. "You mentioned earlier in the car about Kayla's boyfriend coming to town. When's that happening?"

"Oh, yeah. Matt's coming to town in a couple of weeks."

"How do you feel about that?"

My lips tightened. My mind was still on his business trip coming up.

"That bad, eh?" He said, bringing his ice water to his lips. After taking a sip, he set it back down. "I bet teenagers are difficult to raise."

"Yeah. They can be a handful at times. Today's world doesn't help."

"Right? I couldn't be a teenager these days." He shook his head. "They've got to deal with constant bombardment from every direction. Social media, friends, schools, teachers, parents, the internet.

When I was growing up, there was Mom and Dad and maybe the library, if you lived close to one or were able to find a ride."

My mind let loose of the business meeting and engaged him in the conversation. "I know! Now they have all this information at their fingertips and think they know *everything*." I thought of Kayla.

"I will say, though, that Kayla isn't too bad since we moved here. I think moving and only having me around have really been helpful for her."

"That's got to be a relief. I'm happy you decided to take me up on the offer."

My stomach twisted thinking about his trip to Colorado coming up again. I wanted to be happy about the date we were on, about our chemistry we'd had all throughout the day, but it was difficult to hold firmly to the good. I feared he'd break my heart just like Jonathan did. The worst part of it all was that I had actually convinced myself I had been fully healed from Jonathan—I hadn't. The worry overwhelmed me to the point of a stomachache.

"I don't feel so good. Can we wrap up here and you take me home?"

He looked bewildered. "Sure. Let me grab the check and we'll go."

CHAPTER 24-HANNAH

LUKE GOT OUT OF HIS car and walked me to my door.

"It was nice getting to know you more. I think what you're doing for yourself and your daughter by moving out here is great."

"Thanks." I felt thankful he didn't mention the awkwardness I most likely exhibited at the restaurant. "I had a good time too, Luke."

He stuck out a hand.

Odd, I thought to myself as I shook his hand.

"Have a good night."

He turned and went out to his car and I went inside.

Setting the Zantac down on the kitchen counter, I peered over at Kayla's bedroom door and saw the light was off. She had already gone to sleep.

Going over to the stove, I pulled the tea kettle off the back burner and filled it half-way with water. As I set it back on the burner and turned the heat to high, I recalled how I'd felt when Luke had helped me hold the gun out in the woods that afternoon. His arms around mine, his hands touching mine. I hadn't been that close to a man in years, and I liked it.

Continuing into the living room, I lay down on that old red stitched couch and let my mind dwell more on the day's events with him. We were waiting for a table at the restaurant earlier on a bench when he leaned over to me to say something. When his breath tickled my neck, it sent a shiver down the length of my spine.

The tea kettle whistled.

Arising from the couch, I went back into the kitchen and pulled it off the burner, then fetched a mug and tea packet from the cupboard. Pulling down the blue mug that was Jonathan's, all the insecurities I had felt earlier in the evening flared. *Why'd I keep this stupid thing?* I wondered as I broke down.

Tears started to flow as I became increasingly worried about becoming attached to Luke. I liked him already, and that worried me.

With tears still in my eyes, I finished making my cup of tea and took it with me into my bedroom.

Setting the cup down on my nightstand, I went into the bathroom to remove my makeup.

As I used a makeup remover pad and peered into the mirror, I felt a tug-of-war raging inside me. One side was pulling toward wanting to pursue a relationship with Luke, and the other side didn't want anything to do with the guy. Praying, I asked, "How am I supposed to know what You want me to do? I can't see Your will clearly, Lord. Help me, please. Amen."

I shut the light off and went to my bed. Getting beneath the covers, I reached over to my nightstand, flipping on the lamp, and grabbed my tea. Snuggling up with my back against the backboard, I pulled my Bible from the pillow beside me and began to read in John.

CHAPTER 25-HANNAH

AFTER MAKING MAC BREAKFAST THE next day, I picked up the dirty laundry in his room as he ate.

"How was my son?"

Resting the laundry basket on my hip, I paused and nodded. "He seems like a nice guy."

"You put him in the friend zone."

I laughed. "Not necessarily. I'm just getting out of a divorce."

"I thought that was two years ago."

"Yeah, it was two years ago, but so what? You can't put a time frame on healing."

"You're just an eagle living with a bunch of chickens."

"What?"

"You can fly, but you won't spread your wings and give it a shot. You'd rather stick with what's comfortable."

Ignoring him, I continued to pick up the laundry, but with a frustration to how I conducted myself, throwing each piece forcefully into the basket. Mac didn't know what he was talking about. He hadn't been there when Jonathan broke my heart and my daughter's.

I stopped.

"I'm not going to keep quiet. You know what, Mac? You don't understand the pain I went through when my husband left me and my daughter. Your wife died and is gone, but she loved you till her last breath. My husband willingly left us and chose not to love us." Covering my mouth as shock rippled through me at my lack of self-control, I quickly followed it up. "Sorry. I shouldn't have said that."

"No, don't be sorry. You were being real—I like that. You can be mad at me if you want, but you know I'm right. I know my son and he's a good man. I understand you were hurt in a way I nor any other guy will ever understand, but living in fear is no way to live."

"I have to go toss this in the washer and get ready for church. Have a good morning, Mac."

Venturing back to the guest house, I pushed aside the conversation with Mac, but I did take note of his kind words about his son. Mac didn't seem to care about anyone, and the fact that he mentioned goodness with Luke meant something. Arriving inside the guest house, I found Kayla was already completely dressed, her makeup and hair done, and sitting on the couch with her Bible on her lap.

"Wow. Look at you, being a good little church girl."

"Mac said to me the other day that if I want a better life, I have to plant seeds."

I thought to myself, *of course he did, and you, of course, listened to him.* Clearing my annoyance, I said, "I thought you were worried about people finding out about the pregnancy?"

"I am a little worried about that, but I can't let it stop me. God loves me, and I have to hope His people will too."

"God's a bit kinder to us than we are to each other."

"Oh." Her countenance fell.

Walking over to the couch, I sat down beside her and draped an arm over her shoulders. "Listen. I love you, but I'm not going to be able to protect you against what people will say or how they will feel. But I will stand by your side, no matter what."

"I know." Her tone dripped with sadness I felt I had put there by my own words.

"But you know what, dear? God is going to work this all out for good. Just watch."

She nodded. Wiping a few stray tears running down her cheeks, she looked me in the eyes. "You have to be open also, Mom. I heard you crying last night in the kitchen."

My heart was troubled. I didn't mean for her to hear me. I thought she had already fallen asleep.

"I'm sorry you heard that. I didn't mean to worry you."

Looking me in the eyes, she shook her head. "Don't ever be sorry for crying, Mom."

"Okay. I'm going to go get ready for church." I stood up and headed to my bedroom to get ready for church. Mac's words railed against my thoughts, pushing me, pulling at me. The tug-of-war inside of me was consuming my thoughts. Halfway through dressing, I stopped and sat on my bed to pray. Praying was like air in my life—a necessity I couldn't live without.

CHAPTER 26-HANNAH

PASTOR CHARLIE STOOD AT THE pulpit, not merely just the man who had helped me with moving into the guest house on Mac's ranch, but a man of God who spoke the power of truth into the lives and hearts of his congregation. While he was the same individual who had been out on the ranch helping, he carried himself differently when he was up preaching the Word of God.

Picking up his handkerchief from beside his Bible on the pulpit, he wiped his brow as he paused his words. The heater was busted on the max position in the church that morning, and even though both doors in the sanctuary were wide open, it wasn't enough to cool the room's temperature to a suitable level. After wiping the sweat from his forehead, he walked down the steps of the stage. He surveyed all of our faces as we waited for him to continue to speak.

"Joseph's brothers," he said, shaking his head. "His brothers did an evil thing. They wanted to hurt him by doing it too." He paused again, then walked up the steps back to the pulpit and to his open Bible. He leaned over the pages and read aloud. "In Genesis 50:20, it says, '*You intended to harm me, but God intended it for good to accomplish what is now being done, the saving of many lives.*'"

He peered up from the Bible and grabbed hold of the pulpit on both sides as he raised his voice. "This man, Joseph, is a man of character, a man of depth, and he truly held a Godly perspective. How often do we in our own lives have the mindset that what we are going through is just *too hard*? How often are we guilty of thinking that our lives aren't fair?" Raising his eyebrows, he paused. "Listen, I'm preaching to myself this morning probably more than I am preaching to you. I've been there! When those stinking thieves kept robbing our lumber from the construction site of our church, I was furious. The other week, when I heard about the school shooting or last month, about the church getting shot up, I was irate! Ladies and gentlemen, I'm not here to tell you that this world is wicked. You can see it for yourself. It's full of evil. But God's works can and do work all things together for good for those who love Him and are called according to His purpose. Joseph has the right mindset here in the Scriptures. He understands, and it's not because he hasn't suffered, but it's because he *has* suffered that he truly understands and holds this Godly perspective. Our Savior was nailed to a cross. Right? You think they intended it for harm? You bet they did, but God intended it for *good.* God's in control when our life seems to be out of control."

My heart was beating like a drum in my ears. God wasn't surprised when I learned of Jonathan's other family. He also wasn't surprised when I learned of Luke's similar job that took him out of town. I was beginning to realize that maybe God set this up in this way in order to show me, to grow me.

On the way out of the service, as we headed to the car, Kayla asked, "How was Charlie's preaching?"

"Good. How was youth group? Did you make some friends?"

She laughed a little. "Mom. We're not a bunch of little kids who just become friends after two seconds. It went well though." She smiled. "They were all really nice and I even broke the ice about being pregnant. I wanted it out of the way, and while I was terrified to tell them all . . . they received it well and I didn't feel judged over it."

"Wow, I'm impressed you put yourself out there like that. I'm proud you got it out there. Now you don't have to worry about it."

She smiled. "Thanks."

As we left the church parking lot, I thought of the lunch I was about to make for Mac. I pondered the idea of sharing a side of truth along with his sandwich. In my heart, I knew he needed that message I heard just as much as I did. I just wasn't sure if his heart would be open to it.

CHAPTER 27-HANNAH

MY NERVES FLARED AS I walked down the hallway to Mac's bedroom with his sandwich on a plate and a message on my heart. He wasn't easy to talk to, and our last exchange wasn't exactly heartwarming, but I had been searching for a way to share more of my faith with him and I felt today's message at church was the open pathway to doing just that.

Setting his plate down on his lap, he peered up at me.

"What's on your mind, child?"

I backpedaled in my mind about talking to him. "Oh, nothing. Just today's message. It was really good and powerful."

He was curious and asked, "What was it?"

This was it, my ticket to sharing. Though I had thought about the moment over the last couple of days and desired it, I suddenly found myself frozen with inaction. I had envisioned myself pacing around his room and sharing God's truth and love with him and then him falling to his knees in repentance to God. What actually happened was far different. I was timid. Softly, I said, "God is in control even when everything is a mess in our life."

"Hmm. And?"

The frost thawed within me and God loosened my lips. I sat down on the end of his bed and turned my body toward him. "Charlie talked about Joseph and how his brothers intended to harm him, but how God worked it for good. I thought a lot about my own life and everything that happened with Jonathan. I was devastated, but God already knew it all along."

"Yeah, and he didn't even warn you." He sarcastically laughed. "Sounds like a great God."

Shaking my head, I could see the brokenness of Mac's heart in the moment. "Mac, it's horrible what happened to Rita. I could never imagine how it'd feel to lose your best friend to something like cancer. Jonathan and I were a sad situation, but we were never best friends in my mind. I don't think he ever loved me the way you loved Rita. But listen." I leaned toward him and rested a hand on the covers. "God brought you in my daughter's and my life for a reason, and I have to believe that. God is always working, Mac, and I know you know that. You can be hard and resistant to God and act like you don't care, but you're looking forward to Heaven with Him. You said it yourself."

His expression softened. "It just hurts that He didn't save her. I felt lost after she passed away. He took away my best friend!"

"God didn't kill your wife, Mac. Yes, He let her come to Him, but you have to know that she was already His to begin with."

Wiping a tear from his cheek, he let out a sigh. "I know. She was never truly mine to begin with . . ." Swallowing, he looked to the window. "I don't think God has anything more for me to do."

"But you're already doing something."

He looked over at me, confusion written across his expression.

"You and Kayla. She needs a father figure in her life, and you're doing it."

He laughed a little. "I'm barely talking to her, and it's just a bunch of little nuggets of common sense."

"Common sense she's listening to. You know she went to church this morning because of something you said?"

He raised his eyebrows, a slight smile on his lips. "She did?"

"You told her about planting seeds. That was another Biblical reference from you. I can see right through you, Mac. Your boys might not, but I do. You try to put up this front of being hard and mean and angry at God, but you can't get away from the Truth you know in your heart."

"I'm glad she went." His eyes turned to his sandwich and he continued. "Now leave before my food gets cold."

I smiled, knowing a sandwich was cold to begin with.

"Okay."

Rising from his bed, I knew I had done the right thing, and I praised God on my way out of Mac's house that afternoon.

Walking over to the side of the house, I grabbed the hose and headed over to the garden. Though the seeds hadn't sprouted through the soil yet, I knew there was growth going on beneath the surface. Walking along each row, I watered, knowing my efforts would pay off in the weeks and months to come.

CHAPTER 28-LUKE

AT ABOUT FOUR O'CLOCK THAT Sunday afternoon, I called Hannah. Though I had seen her all day on Saturday, I couldn't get her out of my mind. My leftovers from last night became my lunch, but there was a crucial missing ingredient— her. Remembering she had mentioned an internet issue with their computer, I finally made the call.

"Hey." She had a way of saying even the simplest word with a delightful tone of voice.

"Hey, it's me, Luke."

"I know who it is." She laughed. "What's up?"

"I just remembered you mentioning something with the internet last night, and we didn't really set up a time for me to fix it."

"How about now?"

I smiled. She wanted to see me just as much as I wanted to see her. "Okay, I can do now."

"I'll make you dinner, as a token of my appreciation."

"Mmm. My dad tells me you're a pretty good cook. What's for dinner?"

"Shrimp jambalaya. It's an old family recipe."

"Mmm . . . spicy?"

"Yes."

"Sounds great. I'll head out now."

Hanging up with Hannah, I hurried out the door and to the ranch. On the way out to the ranch, I started to envision a future where she and I were officially dating. But doubts swarmed my mind. I hadn't yet told her about Pamela or that I can't have children. These things were important, I knew that, but I didn't think they really needed to be brought out into the open quite yet. We were still getting to know each other.

I called Victor on my car speaker system while I drove.

"Pamela."

"Don't like that name."

"No. Do I tell Hannah about her?"

"Of course you tell her, but you wait until the third date. That way, she has a chance to like you before she finds out about the wicked witch of the past."

"Hiding it doesn't sit well with me though."

"That's because you're a nice guy, but what do they say about those nice guys? They finish last. Dead last. Keep your mouth buttoned."

"Remind me again—why do I take so much advice from you?"

"Because I was right about Pamela and you didn't heed my words."

"Ouch. That was rhetorical."

"Sorry, brother. Hey. I'm at a baseball game though. I have to let you go."

"All right. Take it easy."

Hanging up with him, I shut the radio off and prayed for guidance. "God, help me. You steer this car called my life and show me the path You want to go down. Show me Your way. Enable me to walk by sight and to speak when I should speak and keep quiet when I should keep quiet. You're the One who leads me. Amen."

Pulling into the driveway out at the ranch, I came under the shade of the trees hanging over the road and caught sight of Hannah's daughter sitting by my father on his front porch. It made me glad to see him doing something other than reading westerns or watching re-runs of MASH in his living room. He needed to get outside more and enjoy the country living that was only a few feet from his bed.

CHAPTER 29-HANNAH

SITTING DOWN TO THE TABLE over at Mac's, we bowed our heads and Luke led us in prayer.

"Bless this food we're about to partake, Lord. Thank You for providing us not only with this food, but with each other's company and this time together. Please heal my father's body and help his wounds on his legs to bind up. We also ask for a special blessing on the preparer of this food. Amen."

Lifting my spoon, I brought my first bite to my lips and blew on it.

"Wow. This is amazing soup," Mac said with delight.

Luke turned to his dad. "Wow. I've made you food for years without as much as a thank you."

Mac shrugged, then let out a light laugh. "Maybe it wasn't ever good. Did you think of that?"

"My mom got this recipe from my grandma Beatrice before she passed away. My dad always loved it."

"How was church?" I asked, my gaze locked on Luke.

"Good. It was baptism Sunday. Twelve and a half people were baptized."

"Half?" Mac asked, pausing his spoon at his lips. "How on earth does half a person get baptized?"

We all laughed.

Luke continued. "There was a kid, about five, who was baptized outside the water. They just did it alongside the tub of water."

"What? Why?" Kayla asked.

"He's allergic to the chlorine that is in the water."

"So then he's not saved, right?" Kayla asked.

"Dear," I said, reaching over and touching her hand, "It's not the water that saves you. You were saved before you entered the water."

"Your mother is right," Luke added. "The water is symbolizing the redemptive work and transformation that already happened. It's an outward declaration. A symbol."

"Oh, I see."

Mac joined in. "Some religions out there think the water is what saves you, but it's not the water. It's the blood of Jesus that saves us."

My heart warmed at the words of these two men sitting at the dinner table. Jonathan would never speak of God. Sure, we went to church, but that was about it when it came to Jonathan's relationship with God. I guess that made it easier for him to carry on with his other family, keeping God in a nice little box on Sunday morning.

"Matt believes there are multiple ways to get to heaven. He thinks it's not fair that God would only make one way."

Mac shook his head. "Your boyfriend is an idiot. We shouldn't be upset there is only one way and question it. Instead, we ought to be happy there is a way!"

"Dad." Luke appeared displeased with his slight against Matt.

"No, it's fine," Kayla interjected. "I agree. He's an idiot." Bringing a bite of jambalaya to her lips, she said under her breath, *"A lot, lately."*

I don't think Mac or Luke caught her comment, but I did. It made me wonder what was going on, and I planned to ask her about it later.

After dinner and clean up, Luke and I went for a walk while Kayla stayed with Mac on the porch.

As we walked along the white fence that separated the yard from the fields, I turned to Luke and said, "Mac's really softening up."

He laughed. "Sure, if calling Matt an idiot just highlights his sweetness."

Stopping, I grabbed Luke's hand, stopping him.

He turned to me.

"Your dad is just real." My eyes turned to the porch where Mac and Kayla were sitting. "Kayla's a teenager. She dealt with a lot of fake people in high school back in Flagstaff. She'd come home crying because of this girl saying something behind her back or that girl doing some outrageous thing. Even her dad lied to her and was fake most her life. Mac's just real and straight with her. I think that's refreshing to her."

He turned, and we continued walking the fence. "I guess I've just become calloused over the years. I see him as abrasive and rude."

"He is a little, but he is also a brother in Christ."

He scowled.

"What?"

We stopped again. This time, we climbed the

fence and sat side by side on the top plank.

"I want to believe my dad is a brother in Christ and covered in the blood. I think he knows it all, but his heart . . ."

"Only God can judge the heart. We can only see the outside."

"Yeah, exactly, my point. His outside is quite ugly."

My gaze fell to Mac's porch. "Yeah, a little rough around the edges, but there's fruit. I think he's bitter about losing your mom."

His chin dipped to his chest.

"Sorry."

Lifting his eyes to mine, he shook his head. "Don't be sorry. I know he has a lot of hurt that he hasn't healed from ever since she left this earth." His eyes drifted to Kayla and Mac. "Maybe Kayla's coming here is part of God's plan for my dad."

"Maybe it is."

His eyes peering into mine, he continued. "Maybe your coming here is part of God's plan for *our* lives?"

I smiled, my heart warming at his words. "Maybe it is."

CHAPTER 30-HANNAH

WITHOUT MORE THAN A FEW winks of sleep due to not wanting to go to sleep after another pleasant day with Luke, I finally rolled out of bed to go make Mac breakfast. As I cooked his eggs and bacon, I thought of Luke, about Mac and Kayla, and overall, my life as a whole. I was enjoying the direction it was headed.

Taking Mac's plate of food down the hallway, I pushed open his door.

"Why didn't you tell me?" Mac's words were firm and ready to fire as soon as I opened that door.

"About what?" I walked over to the side of his bed and set down the plate.

"That baby daddy coming to town."

"Oh. Um."

"Is it because of what I said?"

"What did you say?"

"I said I'll shoot any boys who end up on my property."

"I didn't tell you, Mac, because I didn't think you would care that her boyfriend was in town for a few days."

He got really quiet. Then, he said, "I do care about her boyfriend being out here on the ranch. I don't want him here, and I don't think you do either."

"I don't have the energy to fight with you today, Mac. Fighting against a teenaged girl's will is like fighting a brick wall."

Leaving his side, I headed for the door.

"So it's too hard and you just give up?"

Stopping, I turned around. "No, actually, I took some good advice from the pastor's wife."

"Oh, because she has a teenager?"

"Touché."

He shook his head. "If that boy wants to treat your daughter like a used car and you let him just come around whenever he wants and just give in at every angle, you're teaching her that you're fine with her being treated that way. He's garbage."

"She loves him."

"Yeah, sure, and Sally loves George in Chemistry. It's puppy love. It'll die."

"Then why fight it?"

"Because if you don't as a parent, nobody else will. Someday, she'll thank you."

"Thanks for caring for my daughter, but I'll parent her the way I want to parent her."

Walking out of his room, I shut the door and hurried out of his house. This man was impossible to deal with, whether he cared or didn't care, but I couldn't deny the truth behind his words. I just felt stupid.

Kayla was still asleep when I got back to the guest house, so I wrote a note to tell her I went for a drive, leaving out the reason I was upset.

I drove by the church intentionally, wondering if Serenah or Charlie was in. I saw a lone car in the parking lot.

It was white, and a bit beat up.

Pulling into the parking lot, I parked and went inside the church.

Glancing down a hallway, I saw a light on and a door open, so I ventured down that way.

Walking into the office, I saw a man sitting behind the desk of Ed Anderson, the associate pastor of the church, maybe in his early thirties, late twenties.

He looked up.

"Who are you?"

"Hannah. You?"

He laughed sarcastically and tossed the paper in his hands on the desk in front of him. "I'm nobody."

"Okay . . ."

Rising to his feet, he left from behind the desk and walked over to me. "I'm Ed's kid—James. You know, I thought I had more time to quit the drugs. Quit the crazy life before he'd pass on from his heart problems, but . . ." He glanced over at the Bible on the desk and shook his head. "Life happens when you're too busy being selfish."

I was speechless as I recalled the mention for prayer for Ed in the announcements yesterday morning.

Raising his hand, he shook his head. "Sorry. I don't know why I'm sharing all this. I guess you don't know me, so it's easier. Anyway . . . what's up? Why are you here, *Hannah*?"

"I thought maybe Pastor Charlie was in."

He smiled, but it was fake, I could tell. "He's not here, obviously."

Raising a hand, I said, "I've already dealt with one too many rude people today. I'm outta here."

As I got into my car back outside in the parking lot, the kid came running out.

"Hey. I'm sorry. I'm just a druggie who lost his dad." He slowed to a walk as he arrived up to me.

"Can I pray with you?"

He raised his eyebrows, then nodded.

Bowing our heads, I led him in a prayer. "God, You are the sustainer of our souls. We long for You and we need You in our life. I pray for James and I pray You help him. Meet him where he is, like You always do, and show James Your will for his life.

Amen."

We hugged, and he had tears in his eyes.

"You have no idea how much that meant to me."

"Nope, but God does. He loves you, James."

Parting ways, I got into my car. My heart warmed as I received an incoming text message from Luke. It broke away some of the coldness that had settled over my heart earlier that morning. I desired to see him, to apologize for the restaurant the other night. I hadn't done it yesterday, and instead just swept it under the rug like it never happened. I knew I needed to clear the air and be upfront about my insecurities. A relationship couldn't be built on secrets, and I had to let him know my fears.

Calling Kayla, I let her know I was heading into

Spokane.

CHAPTER 31-HANNAH

ARRIVING IN DOWNTOWN SPOKANE, I parked
and fed the meter before heading up to the twenty-
third floor of the Berkley building, where Luke's
office was located. On the elevator ride up, each
floor the elevator passed sent my heartbeat
skyrocketing. There was no way to be certain how
Luke would take the words I was about to tell him,
but I hoped in my heart that he'd be able to receive
them well. I planned to spill my heart out, share my
truth, and hope he'd still be interested in the end.
He could very well end up rejecting me, refusing to
be with someone so insecure, but it was a risk I had
to take.

Ding . . .

Walking out from the elevator, I saw the door

that led into his office. The name *Young's* hung on the outside of the glass door, stenciled in gold. Below the name, the address *Suite 2304b*.

Opening the door, I let myself in.

There was no receptionist behind the desk, but there was a nicely dressed woman sitting in one of the chairs in the lobby. She had long legs, a white dress and coat, along with a long-brimmed hat on. She looked ritzy, part of one of those high societies. Not much of a surprise to see a woman like that in his office. I'm sure he only dealt with the elites of the world, people running businesses that spent more money than most people saw in a lifetime.

I took a seat beside her.

"Who are you?" the woman asked, lifting her chin as she looked me over like a specimen.

"I'm Hannah. A friend of Luke."

Her eyebrows lifted and she removed one of her white gloves, sticking out a hand. "A friend of Luke's? I didn't know Luke had friends. Nice to meet you. I'm Pamela. Luke's wife. How do you know Lukey?"

My heart sank to the ground level of the building. My face went flush.

In shock, I shook her hand. "Oh. Um. I live on the ranch with Mac."

Standing up as I became increasingly uncomfortable as my worst nightmare unfolded before me, I adjusted my purse farther up onto my shoulder. Turning, I headed for the door, but just then, a woman came out from an office door. "Oh, I'm sorry. I didn't hear you come in. Did you have an appointment to see Luke?"

Shaking my head, I hurriedly slipped out the door and back toward the bank of elevators on the far end of the hallway.

My eyes welled with tears as I covered my mouth and stepped onto the elevator.

When the doors shut, I lost all control over my emotions and wept.

Each floor that dinged on the way down brought on another wave of memories of Jonathan. All the pain I had been convincing myself was just insecurity came crashing back into my heart. I didn't cry so much because of the pain Luke had caused, but because of myself falling for another man who had a secret life. I felt like I didn't understand anything anymore. I was hurt and felt lost.

Reaching the car down on the sidewalk, I glanced at the towering skyscraper. I thought of God's kindness and His goodness in letting me find out the truth before we got too far into the relationship. Sure, it hurt, but at least it wasn't fifteen years into a life together. For that, I was thankful.

Getting into the car, I resolved to return my focus on Kayla. I hadn't made the decision to uproot my daughter so I could come fall for a guy who'd break my heart. I came for a fresh start. I knew Luke enough at this point to know he'd leave me alone if I left him alone. I planned to do just that.

CHAPTER 32-HANNAH

AFTER OUR MEAL, WHILE I cleared the table of Mac and Kayla's plates, Mac stopped me.

"You're upset."

Kayla had already gone back to the guest house at this point, so I didn't mind opening up about his son. "I met Luke's wife today."

Raising his eyebrows, he corrected me. "You mean ex-wife? Right? Pamela."

"What?"

"They haven't been together in over a year and a half. She didn't mention that?"

I shook my head, but the news didn't comfort me much. "No, but he didn't mention being married before."

Mac nodded as I took the plates over to the sink.

"He doesn't like talking about Pamela. It's a sore subject."

Forcefully, I set the plates into the sink and turned around. "I don't care if it's a *sore* subject. It should've been mentioned."

Furrowing his eyebrows as he slid the toothpick in his mouth to the other side, he paused, looking me over. "You like my son."

"Liked your son. Yes."

"You telling me you haven't held back any part of yourself from him?"

Mac's words were laced with the chilling reminder that I was on the way there to expose my own secret. "Well, I didn't tell him everything, but I planned on it."

"Maybe he did too."

Shaking my head, I said, "Look. Meeting her was a reality check. I'm here for Kayla and me, not for me finding love. I need to focus on her instead of another reason to be distracted and not at home. I can't deal with a relationship right now."

Raising his hands, he said, "Okay. I wasn't telling you what to do, just being straight with you."

Leaving the kitchen after the dishes, I headed back over to the guest house when I saw Luke's car pulling up the driveway. I couldn't avoid him forever, so I met him out in the driveway.

"Hey. What's going on? You haven't answered any of my texts or calls."

"I met your wife. Ex-wife. Whatever."

His confusion fell away, and sorrow filled his face in the very next second. "I was going to tell you, Hannah. I swear. I was waiting for our third date."

"How convenient for you." Raising my hands, I shook my head. "I wasn't even sure about this to begin with. Honestly, I was on the fence about a 'you and me' and it just helped me realize I need to focus on my daughter. I'm here for my daughter and for myself to have a fresh start. I'm not ready."

"Okay. I'll wait."

Raising an eyebrow, I asked, "What? You'll wait?"

He nodded. "I know we've only spent a small amount of time together, but I haven't ever met someone like you. I know you're worth the wait, and

I'll wait it out. I've been alone for a long time, and I can wait."

"You've only been away from your wife for a year and a half."

"Come on, Hannah. You know just as much as I do that the separation start isn't where the loneliness starts. It's long before then. Regardless, I'll give you the distance you need. I'll give you whatever you need, because I know you're worth it."

My heart warmed at his romantic comment, but I wasn't sure if he'd wait for me. "I don't know when I'll be ready, Luke."

"That's fine. I'll be praying for you and Kayla."

As we parted ways and he got back into his car, I was overwhelmed with emotions ripping inside my chest. He was so understanding and romantic.

Maybe someday, Luke and I could work. Maybe someday, God would bring an 'us' into existence. For now, it was about Kayla and my future grandbaby.

Arriving inside the guest house, I was met with a teary-eyed daughter. Mascara running down her cheeks, she said, "He dumped me and signed over his rights!"

Relieved but saddened at the same time, I pulled her in close, without saying a word, and hugged her. Though we both had lost something that day, we had gained something too—focus.

CHAPTER 33-LUKE

Six and a half months later . . .

SITTING PATIENTLY FOR MY PLANE to make its way down the runway, I stared out the little window of the plane and watched as the snow flurries fell from the mid-December sky. Remembering an important meeting I had scheduled in the afternoon but hadn't put on my calendar, I phoned my receptionist, Cindy.

"Cindy. I just remembered, I had a thing in the afternoon with *Johnson & Henry*. Please call them and reschedule, and also send a gift basket."

"That wasn't on your calendar."

"I know, I know. I forgot to add it when Henry

called, but they were expecting me out at the plant opening today."

"I'll take care of it. This must be some big client if you're willing to shift everything around and fly out a day early."

Nodding, I said, "She is our most important client."

Hanging up with Cindy, I caught the gaze of one of the flight attendants. She was eyeballing me with a glare that burned through my retinas. I knew she was upset I had used my phone shortly before takeoff. I mouthed, 'I'm turning it off,' and then promptly did. Letting out a large sigh, I tried to direct all of my attention on my newest and largest client when my seat partner, an older man with a full head of white hair, sat down and settled in.

"Pleasure or business?"

Raising my eyebrows, I turned to him. "What's the difference when you do what you love every day?"

He laughed and stuck out a hand. "Quick wit, kid. Name's Griff Mackey."

"Luke Frosworth. Nice to meet you, Griff."

"Entertain an old man and tell me what you're up to with your travels."

"I'm flying to Denver to meet with a client."

"What's your line of work?"

"Investment banker." He looked uncertain what it was. I continued. "Basically, I help people make a lot of money."

"You a praying man?"

"Yes, sir."

Placing a hand on my shoulder, he said, "I want to pray over you. If that's all right?"

"Of course."

Bowing our heads, he led.

"God, I want to ask You to help Luke find Your will in his life. We also pray for the meeting to go well with his client. We pray these things in Your name, Amen."

Lifting my gaze, I said, "Thank you. You a pastor?"

He shook his head. "No, not at all. Just a follower of Christ. I felt prompted to pray with you and I try to never ignore a prompting."

"That's a solid philosophy, Griff." Thinking about Hannah, whom I hadn't spoken to but thought of often, I decided to pick his brain since we had a fair amount of time sitting beside each other. I knew seeking counsel was always wise, and I had been thinking of her a lot this afternoon when I had passed a street vendor selling shrimp jambalaya. Over the last six and a half months, I had kept my distance, but I thought of her often.

"Mind if I ask you about something? For advice from one Christian to another?"

He broke into a large grin. "Now this is getting good. What's on your heart, kid?"

"So, there's a girl."

"Of course," he said, slowly nodding and urging me to go on.

"And she's living on a ranch with my dad. We kind of hit it off when we first met, but she needed space after learning about my past and meeting my ex-wife. I'm thinking it's because of past hurts that she's been through that she's kind of hung up on wanting more. I'm just wondering if I should try to pursue her again or not."

"I've been married for over fifty-one years. If there's one thing I've learned about women, it's this. They're emotional and their feelings can change on a dime. God gives us a help-mate, not a robot who does whatever we want them to do. Each of us comes to a marriage with a problem. But it's not what you think. It's not just emotional baggage from previous failed relationships or how they were raised and the results thereof. We each come to marriage as a broken and sin-filled human being. As

217

husbands, it's our job to love our wives like Christ loves the church. That means regardless of the other person's shortcomings. I'm rambling. My apologies. Listen. If you and this gal have the same sort of values when it comes to life, for example, your faith, you ought to talk to her. Maybe she'll come around? You have nothing to lose and everything to gain."

"Wow. That's incredibly insightful. You're a good advice giver."

He raised a hand and shook his head. "No good is within me. It's all Jesus."

I smiled.

I was upset about having to fly out a day early for this meeting, but I realized right then that God knew I'd sit by Griff by leaving a day earlier. Orchestrated with flawlessness, God was piecing together His will in my life. He knew I'd pass by that street vendor and smell that same dish she had made me. Suddenly, I was overwhelmed with His affection for me as I caught glimpses of His hand painting a brush stroke in my life. Immediately, I praised Him and thanked Him for my life.

CHAPTER 34-HANNAH

ARRIVING INSIDE FROM A COLD morning walk on the ranch, Kayla approached me as I removed my gloves.

"Mom, this heartburn is horrible and I'm out of Tums and Zantac. Please go get me more, or I fear I'll die."

"That bad, eh?"

"Yes! I'm so ready to get this little guy out of me." Glancing to the ceiling, she continued. "Any day now, Lord!"

Smiling, I came closer to my daughter and smoothed my hand over her hair. "I think we're all ready. Did you settle on a name yet?"

"Yep. It's Kip."

"That's cute, and I guess I can run to town quickly and get you some medicine. I need to pick up a few things for dinner anyway."

Walking into the kitchen, I grabbed my purse from the counter. "Are you sure you'll be okay alone? What if you go into labor?"

"Geez, paranoid much? You really think a baby would come that fast while you run to a store? First time mom here, and even I know first labors go slow. I'll probably be pregnant for another two weeks at this rate."

Waddling to the recliner, she worked herself into the seat and closed her eyes. Opening them quickly, she turned her head toward me. "Has Mac gotten back yet?"

Mac's other son, Victor, had taken him on a car

trip over to Ocean Shores, Washington, to see the ocean. Mac had convinced him of the trip after he had healed fully from his leg wound months ago. Mac's reasoning for the trip? Kayla told me it was because he wanted to hear the ocean once more before he finally died. He was convinced he was on his way out even if the doctors said otherwise.

I shook my head. "No, they should be back tonight though."

She appeared displeased and let out a sigh. "Okay."

My daughter and Mac had grown close over the months we had been on the ranch. After his leg healed up in early September, they started taking walks together in the fields and continued their evening talks down by the creek. Once it started getting into the colder months, they moved their conversations to the living room by the fireplace in his house. He had become the father she never had, and for that, I was appreciative. Kayla needed a dad in her life, and though her biological father would've been ideal, he wasn't what she got. In the end, it wasn't important who was the father, but that she had someone who could step up to the role. That man had been Mac.

Before leaving, I went into the kitchen and pulled out a freezer bag with a mixed bag of frozen veggies from fall's harvest of the garden. Yelling into the living room where Kayla was still sitting, I asked, "You good with soup tonight?"

"Yeah, that's fine." Her voice sounded a little funny, so I went into the living room and she had her hand on her belly and a grimace on her face.

"Kayla? You okay?"

"Mom, I'm fine. It was just some gas, I think. I'll be a lot better once you get back with that medicine."

Laughing, I kissed her cheek and then proceeded out the door.

On my way to the car, I saw the patch of ground where I knew the garden was, and I thought of Luke. I thought of him every time I passed it. I'd ponder the brief relationship we had for a couple of days last summer. Luke was the first man I had developed feelings for after Jonathan and held a special place in my heart. Though we hadn't spoken more than a few sentences when required since last summer, I still thought of him often and wondered if things would've worked out if I would've given us a try.

Getting to my car, I turned the key over and it wouldn't start. Sighing, I turned the key back to the off position and waited a second. The car had started acting up in October and was in need of a mechanic. Getting it to start the second time, I headed into Newport.

Walking into Fran's Market, I caught the gaze of Bethany, the daughter of the associate pastor Ed, who had passed away, and the sibling to James, whom I had met at the church last summer.

"How are you?" I asked as we embraced. We had become friends through church events and had talked several times about James.

"We're good. Just picking up some groceries. Kayla about to pop?"

"Should be any day now. The heartburn is

getting worse and that's actually why I'm here."

"Heartburn is always worse at the end! Little guy is almost here!"

There was a lingering pain in Bethany that I couldn't see, but I could feel it behind every conversation, sense it in the moments of quiet. I knew she had lost her mother just a couple of years ago, and now her dad was gone too. I couldn't imagine the pain that was associated with losing both parents in such a small window of time. Touching her arm, I said, "How's the family? Any progress on your brother?"

"James is in rehab, again." She tightened her lip and suddenly, I saw her eyes moisten, the pain of her heart poking out. "I have a blessed life, Hannah. I really do, but sometimes . . . it's just hard."

I nodded. "I couldn't imagine."

She stopped and looked at me, tilting her head. "You've been through a lot too, from what you've told me. I always tell myself every person is going through a battle. Sometimes we see it, and sometimes we don't. Thank God we have God through the difficulties!"

"Praise God for that!"

"Amen."

After parting ways with Bethany, I felt encouraged to have seen her at the store. It was people like her, who had been through the worst life had to offer and yet stayed strong in their faith, who made me realize that with God, all things were not only possible, but working together for good.

CHAPTER 35-LUKE

INSTEAD OF STAYING THE NIGHT in Colorado, I decided to fly back that same evening. Griff's conversation with me stuck in my mind throughout my meeting and even prompted me to fly back the same day just so I could go out to the ranch and speak with Hannah. I felt I owed it not only to myself, but to her.

Exiting the airport, I hurried my steps into the parking garage and got into my car.

Loosening my tie, I pulled it off my neck and tossed it into the back seat with my briefcase. Backing out of my parking spot, I put the car into drive and headed out to the ranch.

My phone rang as I was making my way out to the ranch.

It was Victor.

"Brother. I know you're in Colorado tonight, but I had to call you."

"I'm actually on my way out to the ranch. Are you still there?"

"Oh. No, I just left. Why you going out there? What happened to staying in Colorado?"

"I came back early to talk to Hannah."

A long sigh streamed through his end of the call. My brother had coached me after I learned about Hannah finding out about Pamela to leave her alone and let it go. I was turning my back on my brother's advice.

"I know you don't like it."

"Why are you doing it? I thought you were over

this gal, Luke."

Smiling, I said, "I'm not over her. Since the day I met her, I've felt this connection with her and it hasn't ever left me. I met a guy on the plane who made me realize I need to talk to her."

"So you take a stranger's advice over your brother's? Hmm . . . guess I understand where I line up."

There was a long silence, then I asked, "What prompted the call?"

Thankfully, he was able to set the situation aside and redirect his attention to the reason he called. "Oh, yeah. So I was talking to Dad over in Ocean Shores when we were walking the beach."

"Yeah?"

"We were talking about death and that kind of thing, and then I asked him if he had any regrets. He said he regretted how he was with us boys growing up. Wished he could've done better."

My heart flinched. He had always been a difficult man who would never admit he was wrong, but he seemed to have changed.

After a few seconds of silent disbelief, my eyes widened as it sank into the depths of my soul. "Dad said that?"

"Yeah! I was blown away. I've never heard him talk that way before."

"Me either." I wasn't planning on stopping over and speaking with him while I was out there at the ranch, but now I planned on it.

After hanging up with my brother, I arrived at

the ranch.

Pulling into the driveway, I saw Hannah's car wasn't there, so I parked in front of my dad's house.

I let myself in through the front door and began speaking loud enough for him to hear me as I went down the hall.

"Dad. I want to talk to you about something serious."

He didn't reply.

Getting to the door, I paused as it was open and grabbed onto the handle.

"I understand the silent treatment. You've never been big on these kinds of conversations, but I want to say something I haven't said in a long time. I love you, Dad."

A girl's scream came from outside in the backyard, startling me.

Flinging open the bedroom door, I saw he wasn't there.

Turning, I ran.

CHAPTER 36-HANNAH

IN THE AISLE WITH THE heartburn medications for Kayla, I was just placing my hand on the package when my phone rang.

It was Luke.

I answered.

"You have to get back to the ranch now, Hannah!"

His voice trembled, sending worry soaring through me as I dropped the Tums in the aisle.

"What's going on?"

"Betsy was charging to attack Kayla and my dad jumped in the way. The ambulance is on its way, but they only had one available. Kayla is a mess in tears and blood, and her contractions are only minutes apart. I think she's going into labor."

Hurrying out of the aisle, I said, "On my way."

Hanging up, I ran outside and to my car.
Turning the key over, the engine wouldn't start.

Slamming the steering wheel, I looked up at the
ceiling of the car. "Come on, God! A little help!
Please?"

I turned the key over again.

Nothing.

I started to cry.

I called Luke back, and he answered.

"What's wrong?"

"My car won't start!" I pressed my hand against
my forehead. "I don't know what to do. My car won't

start and she's going into labor, Luke!"

"I'll come get you."

"How far apart are the contractions?"

She said in the background, "Four minutes."

"You can't come get me. She needs to go now!"

"I'll take her."

"But your dad, Luke! You have to go with him. Oh, my goodness, I don't know what to do. I'm freaking out!"

"My dad will ride in an ambulance. I can take Kayla. What hospital?"

"Deaconess. And Luke?"

"Yeah, Hannah?"

"Thank you so much. I'll try to figure something

out and meet you at the hospital."

Hanging up with Luke, I got out of my car and ran back into the store. Seeing Paul, the store manager, I hurried my steps over to him as I wiped my eyes of the tears and tried to compose myself.

Grabbing his arm, I said, "Can you give me a ride into Spokane? Kayla's going into labor and my car broke down."

"I can't. My car is with my wife. You know, Mikey is across the street. He's there late working on books tonight. I'm sure he'd give you a lift."

"Okay, thanks!"

Mikey was the owner of the mechanic shop in Newport and was one of the kindest souls around town. Sprinting outside, I ran across the street to the shop's door and pounded on the door frantically.

Lifting my eyes to the evening sky, I prayed.

"God, please let him still be here. Please."

Just then, the door opened.

It was Mikey.

CHAPTER 37-LUKE

HOLDING MY FATHER'S HAND AS we waited for the ambulance, I tried to fight back the tears. He was covered in blood, his own blood, and I could sense death in his immediate future and I was scared. I didn't tell Hannah. I didn't want her to feel bad.

"Sonny boy." My father's words were soft, grizzly with pain as he pushed them out slowly as his back lay firmly pressed against the snow-covered ground.

"Yeah, Dad?" I said, seeing my breath in the cold wintry air.

"I love you. Thank you for giving me a second chance to be a dad."

Shaking my head, I was confused. "What do you

mean?"

His eyes wandered over to Kayla, who was sitting on the picnic bench crying through a contraction. The sound of the ambulance sirens loudened as they rapidly approached up the driveway of the ranch. He motioned for me to come closer, and I leaned in.

"I never wanted those two ladies to live with me in the beginning. But through knowing the two of them, I've been able to experience what love is again. I've been able to be a father in the way I never was to you and your brother."

Pausing, he coughed, and a bit of dark blood dripped from the corner of his lip. He moaned and grabbed his torn open flesh wound on his side.

I swallowed hard and the tears flowed.

He reached up and grabbed the back of my neck,

pulling me in close.

"Love, my son. It's the glue that holds all this thing called life together. God showed me His love over the last six and a half months through that girl. Take care of her and don't let Hannah slip through your fingers. I'll tell Mom 'hi' for you."

The paramedics arrived moments later, hurrying through the snow at the top of the hill and surrounding him as I backed away.

My eyes connected with my dad once more and I said, "I love you."

He smiled, and my heart broke apart knowing I was losing my father. Wiping my eyes, I journeyed over to Kayla.

"Is Mac going to be okay?" Her eyes carried the worry I knew to be true in my heart. I peered over my shoulders at the paramedics who were inspecting the gashes across his chest.

"He'll be okay. One way or another."

She grabbed hold of the frost-covered bench and squeezed. Crying from the pain and unable to speak, she reached out a hand to hold me.

I held her upright.

Once it passed, I said, "How far apart?"

"Three minutes."

"Let's get you to the hospital to have a baby."

Helping her to my car, I helped her into the seat and buckled her.

"Can you grab my tote bag and pull the soup off the stove? The bag is on my bed."

"Sure."

"Get me a cup of soup! I heard they starve women giving birth these days!"

Laughing, I nodded and continued to the guest house.

CHAPTER 38-HANNAH

MIKEY WAS SPEEDING on the highway after we dropped off his new wife in Newport. The delay set us back a few minutes, which irritated me, but I stayed calm. I was thankful for the ride. As we made our way to Deaconess, I kept up with Kayla's progress through texts from Luke.

Mikey and I didn't know each other very well, so there was a bit of awkwardness in the truck. In the hopes of breaking up the quietness between us and also as a distraction, I asked, "How'd you and Tina meet?"

"Oh, great story." He nodded as he smiled over at me. "You know Luke?"

I laughed. "Obviously, you know that I do."

"He helped Tina this last summer. She had broken down on the side of the road and he helped her out. Made sure she got the rest of the way into town and to my shop. After that, it was love at first sight. Honestly, if it hadn't been for him, I wouldn't have met her. No offense to you, but it's the reason I answered my door tonight. I was about to go on a date with her in town."

I couldn't believe what he was saying to me. "Luke helped her?"

"Yep. She hadn't known about Newport being much of a town, let alone having a mechanic. She would've just kept on going if it wasn't for him. I think God had Luke pull over that day and help her, and I'm happy it happened!"

Chills filled my entire being as I thought of the

reality of not having a ride into Spokane if Luke hadn't helped a stranger. Praising God in prayer, I thanked Him for watching out for me and helping me.

Not far from Spokane, the truck began to shake violently.

"What's happening?"

Mikey pulled over.

"What's wrong with it?" I asked frantically. My eyes widened, more upset about the impending birth than I was about his truck breaking down.

"I'm a mechanic, not a vehicle whisperer. I'll have to get out and check under the hood."

"Is it going to take long?"

He looked displeased with my question, his face

grimacing.

"Sorry! I'm just panicking a little bit here."

"Sit tight. Let me check it out."

Getting out of the truck, he went to the front and opened the hood. The whole time, my mind was racing and tears were welling in my eyes. I texted Luke what was going on.

My phone rang—it was Luke.

"No, don't say it!" I demanded.

"She's about to push. Are you almost here?"

The tears broke and the pain of not being with my daughter became too much to handle.

"What's wrong?"

"Really? We're broke down on the side of the

road and my daughter is going to push out little Kip without me there! That's what's wrong, Luke! That's what's wrong! Let me talk to her, please."

He gave the phone to her.

"Mom? I'm okay. Luke's here, and everyone is very nice."

My eyes watered. "Everything is going to be okay. I know we didn't see this coming, but—"

"God did." She had finished my sentence in a different direction than I was going.

"You're right, He did. I'm going to get up there soon. I promise."

"It's okay, Mom. I know everything is going to work out." She paused, letting out a painful breath. "Ouch! Here's Luke!"

Luke came back on the phone. "I'd better get off here."

My breathing in short spurts, I said, "Okay. Take care of my little girl."

Tossing my phone on the seat, I got out of the truck and ventured down the side of the road and out a few yards into the frost-covered field nearby. My heart was heavy, and my eyes couldn't stop the continuous flow of tears running down my cheeks.

"Why, God? Why?"

I looked up at the stars hanging in the night sky as hopelessness filled me. "I try to do what You want me to do and the worst possible thing just keeps happening! Maybe Mac was right. Maybe You don't care." Immediately, I took it back. "I'm sorry, Lord. I am at the end of myself and I cannot fathom what is going on."

A verse surfaced to my heart, one from Proverbs. *His ways are not our ways.*

Nodding, peace began to fill me, the peace of God. The storm raging in my soul quieted as I prayed, and the peace grew.

Another piece of Scripture came to me.

Be still and know that I am God.

My heart was hurting, but I had the peace of the Lord and the joy of the Lord within me.

CHAPTER 39-LUKE

WIDE-EYED AND SLIGHTLY LIGHTHEADED, I took the newborn baby into my hands from the doctor who handed him to me. They had let me cut the cord. The experience was a surreal moment. I never felt emotional hearing a baby cry before, but his first breath of air, the first cry of his life, had me in tears. Holding him now, I felt like I could break him if I made an unexpected movement. My heart raced as my eyes watered, looking at the new life in my hands. A brand-new, tiny life. Moving closer to Kayla, I handed him to her and she pulled him onto her chest.

She beamed with a smile like I had never seen before on her face. Gently brushing her fingertips across his eyes, she leaned in and kissed his forehead.

I had never been in a delivery room before. Sure, I had visited the hospital when Victor's wife had their three kids, but I hadn't dreamed of being there in the delivery room. I used to dream of it, though, under different circumstances, of course. I dreamed of the day Pamela would give birth to a child, but that dream died long ago.

The doctor and the nurses moved around the room with purpose, one of the nurses taking the baby to go clean him up.

As the room cleared, I came close to Kayla. "You're going to be an amazing mom, I can already tell."

She smiled, then it fell away as she looked toward the window in the room. "He is amazing, and I love him more than I love myself already. I can't wait until my mom sees him. Where is she?"

"She's on her way." Though I didn't know how true that statement was, I knew she'd be there soon, one way or another.

"How's Mac?"

My heart dipped into my stomach at the sound of my father's name and the look in her eyes. I knew she cared about him deeply. There wasn't an easy way to break the news to her about Mac's most likely fate, so I neglected to inform her.

"I'll go find out now that you're done delivering. If that's cool?"

"Please do. The nurses are here for me and my son."

Taking my leave from the labor and delivery floor, I headed down to the E.R. to go find out if my father had passed away. Though I couldn't know for certain, my gut told me he was already gone. Finding the receptionist desk, I approached.

"He's in room 24 in ICU. Down the hall to the right."

Surprised to hear that he was still alive, I raised an eyebrow. "Okay."

Coming to the doorway of my dad's room, I peeked in. The room was dimly lit, machines and monitors all around his bed keeping him alive. Then there, in the midst of the darkness and the one small light that hung above the hospital bed, I saw the faint outline of my brother, Victor. He was sitting beside the bed in a chair. He was holding one of our father's hands in both of his.

I entered the room.

"Brother."

He stood up and walked over to me, immediately throwing his arms around my neck. We hugged.

"He's going to die, brother. Our dad's going to die. They said the machines are the only thing keeping him alive, and we both know his feelings on machines."

"I know." My tone was somber, matching my brother's level.

"What happened?" Victor asked, glancing over at our dad.

"Betsy happened. Kayla told me in the car that

they were down by the creek, talking and catching up after Mac's trip, as she had become too warm in the guest house, and he ran inside to grab a refill on their hot cocoa when she screamed. He ran outside and jumped in front of Betsy just as she was about to pounce."

Victor covered his mouth as he peered over at his dad. "He gave his life up for her."

I nodded.

Then we cried and embraced again.

CHAPTER 40-HANNAH

AN UBER RIDE, GENEROUSLY PAID for by Mikey, got me to the hospital. I knew it was too late, but at least I had made it. Hurrying inside, I went straightway to the Labor and Delivery floor of Deaconess.

When I turned the corner and came into the room, I saw my daughter holding her son. All the worry and pain of the difficulties prior to right then melted away.

"Aww . . ." I said, approaching her bed.

She smiled over at me. "He's perfect, Mom."

My eyes watered, and I agreed with a nod. Kayla handed him to me to hold.

Taking little Kip into my hands, my heart warmed. "Hi, little guy. I'm your grandma. Sorry I was late, but I promise I will be better in the future!"

Looking at my daughter while I was holding my grandson, I couldn't think of a better moment in my life. This was truly a moment of one of the purest forms of love, a moment created by God. In a world full of so much pain and hurt, moments in which everything seems right in the world are not only rare, but divine in nature. I praised God and thanked Him.

"Your boyfriend is amazing, Mom. You have to marry him."

I laughed, breaking myself out of the moment, and looked up at her. "Yeah? Where is he?"

"Went to find out more info on Mac. I hope he's

okay. It was so heroic what he did. He jumped in front of the bear and shoved it away."

"What on earth were you thinking, being outside forty weeks pregnant anyway, Kayla?"

"I was hot, really hot. And the heartburn, ugh, I just had to get out of the guest house. And I needed to hear about Mac's trip. I missed him. I hope he's okay. Mac is a good man and means a lot to me."

"I hope so also. He really came around from the grump we met."

"He really did."

We visited for a while more until Luke came into the room. He only stood in the doorway but didn't enter. Turning to him, I saw his eyes were puffy, red, and swollen. Something was wrong with Mac. I knew it.

"I'll be back," I said to Kayla and leaned over to her to kiss her forehead.

Walking out into the hallway to talk with Luke, I turned the corner and immediately, he hugged me tightly.

"Mac's going to die, Hannah. We're pulling the plug tomorrow morning at seven."

My heart jerked. "Seriously?"

Releasing from our embrace, he nodded. Wiping his eyes, he said, "It's in his will not to be on life support. He's always hated the idea of machines keeping him alive, and the doctors said it's the only way." His eyes glanced over my shoulder. "Should we tell her? Or is it too soon?"

I paused for a long time, debating it within me. "Yes, it'll be hard for her, but she should get the chance to say something before he goes. If that's okay with you and Victor."

"Yeah, that's totally understandable. She's the reason I got a chance to see my dad happy again. Be there tomorrow morning around six thirty, and we'll all say something."

His face was downcast. He looked sad. Taking a step closer to him, I lifted his cheeks between my hands.

"You did amazing by staying with Kayla. Thank you."

Leaning up on my toes, I kissed his cheek.

He took a step closer to me and brought his hand up to my cheek, and he leaned in, then kissed me.

Warmth sizzled over my entire body.

We stopped kissing and he peered into my eyes.

"I'm sorry for not doing that sooner."

"You're forgiven."

We both smiled.

"I felt incredibly blessed to be there for Kayla today. A once in a lifetime opportunity since I can't have kids. By the way, I can't have children. I failed to mention that last summer when we were getting close, and I'm sorry about it. I understand if you don't want to be with someone like that. Kids are pretty important."

Shock poured through me at first, but then a calmness I knew that could only come from God led me to speak the words that came from my lips. "I have a darling daughter, and now a grandson. I don't want more children, and if that changes, there's always adoption. Right now, I just want you, Luke. If you'll have me—well, all of us, really. I come as a package deal."

"It's all I've wanted since I've laid eyes on you. That's the truth!"

"Speaking of truth, I need to be honest with you. Your job taking you out of town freaked me out last summer. I can't promise I'll be fine with that even now, but I want to trust you. I really do, and it's not fair to hold Jonathan's trespasses against you."

"I understand." He grabbed my hands in his as he continued. "You were hurt, and I'll do whatever you need me to do to make you more comfortable with the trips. Call you in the evenings when I'm out of town, maybe even bring you with me. Of course, you can have your own separate hotel room, but whatever you need."

"That's sweet, but it's not fair to you. You shouldn't have to deal with my being insecure when you did nothing wrong."

He smiled. "If that's what you need to be more comfortable and for us to work, I'm more than willing to give it to you."

I was overwhelmed by his affection for me and I kissed him again. A baby's cry broke the romantic spell between us.

"Hey, Kayla doesn't want that soup, if you're hungry. It's made with the veggies from the garden."

"Sounds good. I'm famished. Once I get done with the soup, I'm heading back to my dad."

"Of course."

Walking back into Kayla's hospital room, he placed his arm around the small of my back and welcomed tremors of pleasure traveled up my back.

CHAPTER 41-LUKE

VICTOR, MYSELF, HANNAH, Kayla, and even little Kip all crowded around my father's bedside early the next morning. We all said a small something, but it was Kayla's that was the most heart-wrenching of them all.

With tears streaming down her face and her baby in her arms, she spoke. "I'm naming him Mac instead of Kip, and that's because I want him to have your name. In only six and a half months of knowing you, you showed me what the love of a father really means. It wasn't biological, or even step, but it was by choice that you loved me like a daughter. You had every reason in the world to show me hate. I was sixteen and pregnant and naïve, and yet you took the time to sit with me. Took the time to talk and listen."

My heart couldn't help but cleave toward desiring my father to stay alive longer. I never knew him the way Kayla did, and I hurt more for her loss than I did my own.

She continued to speak after pausing to wipe tears.

"You weren't like *my* father to me. You actually cared. You would listen to me go on and on about how stupid Matt was, but you'd always be sure to tell me what you thought after I got done talking." She laughed, prompting the rest of us in the room to laugh. Grabbing hold of his hand, she leaned in closer. "You were the father I never had, and I'll never forget you. I believe God's love showed through you daily, and I want my son to grow up and be the man I know you are, Mac. I know you're happier now, with Rita, so I'll try not to cry so much down here. But instead, I'll remember all the good. I love you, Mac. Thank you for more than you'll ever know."

The doctors and nurses came into the room a few minutes later and began the process of shutting down the machines. Overwhelming sadness tore through me and I stepped out into the hallway. Leaning my back against the wall, I looked up at the tiled ceiling of the hospital hallway and prayed for God to help me.

A few moments later, Hannah appeared in the hall.

"He gone?"

She didn't speak, but she frowned and I knew.

Touching my arm, she said, "He's with Jesus now, Luke. At least we can take comfort in that fact."

She came closer and leaned in, wrapping her arms around me.

Lifting my arms, I embraced her and wept. Losing my father was difficult, but having Hannah there brought a measure of comfort to my soul.

CHAPTER 42-HANNAH

SIX MONTHS LATER, IT WAS June, and Luke and I decided to extend the size of the garden. I had since moved out of the guest house and into the main living quarters, letting Kayla and Mac live in the guest house so I didn't try to control her every mothering task. Kayla and little Mac walked the short distance daily to see me and had all their meals with me too. She had grown up a lot since having Mac. Babies tended to do that to a person, no matter the age. Mac had left the house to Kayla in his will.

We had already tilled a huge lot of ground and put up a fence to keep deer out last weekend, and this weekend, we were planting seeds. Halfway through the afternoon, we took a break. We sat with sweat pouring from our brows as we downed bottles of water feet away from the garden.

Getting up from the place I was sitting, I came over to him and sat on his lap. Putting my arms around him, I looked into his eyes and planted a kiss on his lips.

"What's that for?" he asked.

"It's for you being you. Even when you're covered in sweat and dirt, you're still cute."

"Yeah? Well you look like a hot mess."

Playfully smacking him, I said, "Jerk."

He laughed, then I laughed. A second passed and then he leaned in, nibbling lightly at my neck. Then he moved up to my lips and kissed me.

Suddenly, Kayla came out of the guest house

with Mac in his car seat, and I rolled out of Luke's lap so it wouldn't be weird.

"Good progress, you two!" Kayla smiled at us as she walked toward our old car that Luke had fixed up for her. "I'm going out with Alex. We're taking Mac to a park and then going to a youth group thing over at the pizza parlor."

"What can a baby do at a park?" I asked. "Plus, it looks like it might rain."

She laughed. "I'll bring a coat. As far as what he'll do . . . I think he likes seeing and hearing the other kids."

"All right, dear. Be home by seven."

"I know. Do you work tomorrow? Mac has an appointment." After Mac had passed away, I found a job at a retirement community. It was hard work, but very rewarding and only a short drive into Newport.

"No, I'm off today and tomorrow."

"Okay, great."

She got herself and the baby into the car, then drove off. Luke had his gaze locked on the sky and the clouds hanging above us. He looked to be deep in thought.

Touching his shoulder, I wanted to know what was going on in his head. "Tell me exactly what you're thinking right now."

He smiled and turned to me. "Marry me?"

It began to rain.

My heart overwhelmed with joy, and as rained soaked me, I kissed him.

Two words, one phrase that contained the power to change lives. Words that shape entire lives and words that can bring a grown man to his knees. They are words that, when brought together, can bring immense joy or a deep sorrow to the soul. When Luke uttered those very two words, a little over a year after meeting and six months after we started dating, I knew all of our lives were about to change again.

The End.

Dear Reader,

I hope you enjoyed *When It Rains by T.K. Chapin*, and that it encouraged you in your own personal walk with the Lord. You'll find further inspiration and encouragement on The Potter's House Books website, and by reading the other books in the series. Read them all and be encouraged and uplifted!

Find all the books on Amazon and on The Potter's House Books website.

Book 1: The Homecoming, by Juliette Duncan

Book 2: When It Rains, by T.K. Chapin

Book 3: Heart Unbroken, by Alexa Verde

Book 4: Long Way Home, by Brenda S Anderson

Book 5: Promises Renewed, by Mary Manners

Book 6: A Vow Redeemed, by Kristen M. Fraser

Book 7: Restoring Faith, by Marion Ueckermann

Books 8 – 21 to be announced

Did you enjoy the book?

Leave A Review!

T.K. Chapin

BOOK PREVIEW

Love's Return

Prologue

THE FIRST TIME I LAID eyes on Kirk was back in our senior year of High School while I was walking the track with Chloe. He was beneath the bleachers lip-locked with Vicky Haggar from the cheerleading squad. This wouldn't have been an issue outside of the fact that he was dating my best-friend, Chloe. Not exactly a best first impression.

Two years later when I was twenty, I decided to relocate from Albany, New York, to Spokane, Washington. Kirk had found out about the big journey across country through mutual friends and approached me about road tripping together. I quickly rejected him.

When he offered to pay for all the gas, I couldn't help but give in. With over 2,000 miles to reach Spokane and a strong desire not to rely on my parents anymore, I knew his gas money would help me in the long run. I was on my way to Spokane to stake a claim in my independence from my parents and to work at a software company as a receptionist. Kirk had been into hockey and hoped for a chance at the big leagues by trying out for the Spokane Chiefs.

Through the long journey across the country, somewhere between Buffalo and Cleveland, I suspect, Kirk and I became friends. During our time together on the road, we laughed about Mrs. Bovey, our ninth-grade English teacher who hated children far too much to be teaching them in a school. We also shared our hopes and desires for the future.

When we finally arrived in Spokane five days after

we left our hometown, I not only had a handful of memories from our road trip but a longing for something more for *us*. The trip had given me a chance to see past the façade he had put on in high school and see the real Kirk. At one stop along the way, at a gas station out in the middle of nowhere, he opened my car door for me. Then another time, he grabbed me my favorite candy bar without my even having to ask. When I became tired of driving, he'd willingly take over even if he was tired. Beyond those sweet gestures, I learned of a man who held a lot of regret over his checkered past. He had high hopes to start afresh and make a new life for himself in Spokane. Beneath all the muscles, I found a man with a big heart.

I couldn't give into my desire to see him again, though, or to possibly have a relationship. He was, after all, Chloe's ex-boyfriend. I dropped him off at the bus stop where his friend was picking him up and said

goodbye for what I thought was forever.

Chapter 1-Jessica

FIVE YEARS AND TWO JOBS later, I was on my way to

work when I stopped in at a favorite local coffee shop of

mine downtown, Milo's, for an extra boost of caffeine. I

had already been running late for work as it was,

sleeping through all three of my alarms. There was a

reason to the madness. It was all due to my friend

Isabella, who had kept me up half the night on the

phone. She was like me, single and living on the hopes

of someday being swept away by a gallant gentleman

who would show us the love we needed. We talked last

night about how miserable she was being single in a

world full of married men, the only single ones being

creeps. I understood the pain of loneliness, but only to a

certain degree. My singleness was part of who I was. It

had almost become a friend. Sure, I wanted someone to

love and hold, but I had to trust the fact that God was in control and knew my heart. Plus, I had my work, which filled much of my time.

Standing in the coffee shop near the counter, I waited for my order. I had on my new white pea coat I had just picked up the other day at the mall. When I saw it hanging on the rack on my way through Macy's, I instantly fell in love with it. It went perfectly with my red bucket hat, which I was also wearing. Scrolling through emails on my phone as I waited for my coffee, I felt the pressure of the day catching up with me. Already several new messages. Two from Micah, my boss, one from the graphics department on a design mock-up, and a reply from a pastor I had interviewed a couple of months back. Working at a startup magazine was anything but easy, but I loved every second of it. Not only was I a writer and reporter, but my boss,

Micah's, go-to person for whatever he needed.

Sometimes, it meant donuts and coffee on my way into

work, and sometimes, it meant writing ten articles in

five days and spot-checking the print run at two o'clock

in the morning, four hours before it went to print. It was

hard work, but it carried purpose and I thrived on

purpose.

"Kirk," the barista said behind the counter, setting a

cup down.

It took a moment for the name to register in my

mind, but when it did, my heart leapt as I lifted my eyes

to find the face that went with the name. I didn't think

about him often, but when he did brush across my

thoughts, it was always with fondness for the time we'd

shared together on the car trip five years ago. Over the

years, the man had stayed with me in the depths of my

soul, along with regret. Regret over the fact I hadn't

pursued him the day I dropped him off at the bus stop. We hadn't spent time together before our car ride, but the time we did share over the trip was something special and close to my heart still to this day.

Surveying the coffee shop, I held onto the short string of hope I had carried all these years. It was like a loose thread from a piece of clothing that I knew if I pulled, it would unravel the whole thing. I refused to part with it. There was no certainty that Kirk still lived in Spokane, but it didn't stop me from holding onto the possibility. My friend Chloe, back in Albany, hadn't spoken his name in years, understandably, and I'd never found his name on the Spokane Chiefs' roster (I checked every season), but still . . . I refused to part with the string.

"Thanks," a man said, his voice rugged, worn.

Did you enjoy this sample? Pick it up on Amazon.com!

One Thursday Morning

Prologue

To love and be loved—it was all I ever wanted.

Nobody could ever convince me John was a bad man. He made me feel loved when I did not know what love was. I was his and he was mine. It was perfect . . . or at least, I thought it was.

I cannot pinpoint why everything changed in our lives, but it did—and for the worst. My protector, my savior, and my whole world came crashing down like a heavy spring downpour. The first time he struck me, I remember thinking it was just an accident. He had been drinking earlier in the day with his friends and came stumbling home late that night. The lights were low throughout the house because I had already gone to bed. I remember hearing the car pull up outside in the driveway.

Leaping to my feet, I came rushing downstairs and

through the kitchen to greet him. He swung, which I

thought at the time was because I startled him, and

the back side of his hand caught my cheek.

I should have known it wasn't an accident.

The second time was no accident at all, and I knew

it. After a heavy night of drinking the night his

father died, he came to the study where I was

reading. Like a hunter looking for his prey, he came

up behind me to the couch. Grabbing the back of my

head and digging his fingers into my hair, he kinked

my neck over the couch and asked me why I hadn't

been faithful to him. I had no idea what he was

talking about, so out of sheer fear, I began to cry.

John took that as a sign of guilt and backhanded me

across the face. It was hard enough to leave a bruise

the following day. I stayed with him anyway. I'd put a little extra makeup on around my eyes or anywhere else when marks were left. I didn't stay because I was stupid, but because I loved him. I kept telling myself that our love could get us through this. The night of his father's death, I blamed his outburst on the loss of his father. It was too much for him to handle, and he was just letting out steam. I swore to love him through the good times and the bad. This was just one of the bad times.

Each time he'd hit me, I'd come up with a reason or excuse for the behavior. There was always a reason, at least in my mind, as to why John hit me. Then one time, after a really bad injury, I sought help from my mother before she passed away. The closest thing to a saint on earth, she dealt with my father's abuse for decades before he died. She was a devout Christian, but a warped idea of love plagued my mother her entire life. She told me, 'What therefore God hath joined together, let not man put asunder.' That one piece of advice she gave me months before passing made me suffer through a marriage with John for another five trying years.

Each day with John as a husband was a day full of prayer. I would pray for him not to drink, and sometimes, he didn't—those were the days I felt God had listened to my pleas. On the days he came home drunk and swinging, I felt alone, like God had left me to die by my husband's hands. Fear was a cornerstone of our relationship, in my eyes, and I hated it. As the years piled onto one another, I began to deal with two entirely different people when it came to John. There was the John who would give me everything I need in life and bring flowers home on the days he was sober, and then there was John, the drunk, who would bring insults and injury instead of flowers.

I knew something needed to desperately change in my life, but I didn't have the courage. Then one day, it all changed when two little pink lines told me to run and never look back.

Chapter 1

Fingers glided against the skin of my arm as I lay on my side looking into John's big, gorgeous brown eyes. It was morning, so I knew he was sober, and for a moment, I thought maybe, just maybe I could tell him about the baby growing inside me. Flashes of a shared excitement between us blinked through my mind. He'd love having a baby around the house. *He really would.* Behind those eyes, I saw the man I fell in love with years ago down in Town Square in New York City. Those eyes were the same ones that brought me into a world of love and security I had never known before. Moments like that made it hard to hate him. Peering over at his hand that was tracing the side of my body, I saw the cut on his knuckles from where he had smashed the coffee table a few nights ago. My heart retracted the notion of telling him about the baby. I knew John would be dangerous for a child.

Chills shivered up my spine as his fingers traced from my arm to the curve of my back. *Could I be strong enough to live without him?* I wondered as the fears sank back down into me. Even if he was a bit mean, he had a way of charming me like no other man I had ever met in my life. He knew how to touch gently, look deeply and make love passionately. It was only when he drank that his demons came out.

"Want me to make you some breakfast?" I asked, slipping out of his touch and from the bed to my feet. His touches were enjoyable, but I wanted to get used to not having them. My mind often jumped back and forth between leaving, not leaving, and something vaguely in between. It was hard.

John smiled up at me from the bed with what made me feel like love in his eyes. I suddenly began to feel bad about the plan to leave, but I knew he couldn't be trusted with a child. *Keep it together.*

"Sure, babe. That'd be great." He brought his muscular arms from out of the covers and put them behind his head. My eyes traced his biceps and face. Wavy brown hair and a jawline that was defined made him breathtakingly gorgeous. Flashes of last night's passion bombarded my mind. He didn't drink, and that meant one thing—we made love. It started in the main living room just off the foyer. I was enjoying my evening cup of tea while the fireplace was lit when suddenly, John came home early. I was worried at first, but when he leaned over the couch and pulled back my blonde hair, he planted a tender kiss on my neck. I knew right in that moment that it was going to be a good night.

Hoisting me up from the couch with those arms and pressing me against the wall near the fireplace, John's passion fell from his lips and onto the skin of my neck as I wrapped my arms around him.

The heat between John and me was undeniable, and it made the thoughts of leaving him that much harder. It was during those moments of pure passion that I could still see the bits of the John I once knew—the part of John that didn't scare me and had the ability to make me feel safe, and the part of him that I never wanted to lose.

"All right," I replied with a smile as I broke away from my thoughts. Leaving down the hallway, I pushed last night out of my mind and focused on the tasks ahead.

Retrieving the carton of eggs from the fridge in the

kitchen, I shut the door and was startled when John was standing on the other side. Jumping, I let out a squeak. "John!"

He tilted his head and slipped closer to me. With nothing on but his boxer briefs, he backed me against the counter and let his hand slide the corner of my shirt up my side. He leaned closer to me. I felt the warmth of his breath on my skin as my back arched against the counter top. He licked his lips instinctively to moisten them and then gently let them find their way to my neck. "Serenah . . ." he said in a smooth, seductive voice.

"Let me make you breakfast," I said as I set the carton down on the counter behind me and turned my neck into him to stop the kissing.

His eyebrows rose as he pulled away from my body and released. His eyes met mine. There it was—the change. "*Fine.*"

"What?" I replied as I turned and pulled down a frying pan that hung above the island counter.

"Nothing. Nothing. I have to go shower." He left down the hallway without a word, but I could sense tension in his tone.

Waiting for the shower to turn on after he walked into the bathroom and slammed the door, I began to cook his eggs. When a few minutes had passed and I hadn't heard the water start running, I lifted my eyes and looked down the hallway.

There he was.

John stood at the end of hallway, watching me. Standing in the shifting shadows of the long hallway, he was more than creepy. He often did that type of thing, but it came later in the marriage, not early on and only at home. I never knew how long he was standing there before I caught him, but he'd always break away after being seen. He had a sick obsession of studying me like I was some sort of weird science project of his.

I didn't like it all, but it was part of who he had become. *Not much longer,* I reminded myself.

I smiled down the hallway at him, and he returned to the bathroom to finally take his shower. As I heard the water come on, I finished the eggs and set the frying pan off the burner. Dumping the eggs onto a plate, I set the pan in the sink and headed to the piano in the main living room. Pulling the bench out from under the piano, I got down on my hands and knees and lifted the flap of carpet that was squared off. Removing the plank of wood that concealed my secret area, I retrieved the metal box and opened it.

Freedom.

Ever since he hit me that second time, a part of me knew we'd never have the forever marriage I pictured, so in case I was right, I began saving money here and there. I had been able to save just over ten thousand dollars. A fibbed high-priced manicure here, a few non-existent shopping trips with friends there. It added up, and John had not the foggiest clue, since he was too much of an egomaniac to pay attention to anything that didn't directly affect him. Sure, it was his money, but money wasn't really 'a thing' to us. We were beyond that. My eyes looked at the money in the stash and then over at the bus ticket to Seattle dated for four days from now. I could hardly believe it. I was really going to finally leave him after all this time.

Amongst the cash and bus ticket, there was a cheap

pay-as-you go cellphone and a fake ID. I had to check that box at least once a day ever since I found out about my pregnancy to make sure he hadn't found it. I was scared to leave, but whenever I felt that way, I rubbed my pregnant thirteen-week belly, and I knew I had to do what was best for *us*. Putting the box back into the floor, I was straightening out the carpet when suddenly, John's breathing settled into my ears behind me.

"What are you doing?" he asked, towel draped around his waist behind me. *I should have just waited until he left for work . . . What were you thinking, Serenah?* My thoughts scolded me. Slamming my head into the bottom of the piano, I grabbed my head and backed out as I let out a groan. "There was a crumb on the carpet."

"What? Underneath the piano?" he asked.

Anxiety rose within me like a storm at sea. Using the bench for leverage, I placed a hand on it and began to get up. When I didn't respond to his question quick enough, he shoved my arm that was propped on the piano bench, causing me to smash my eye into the corner of the bench. Pain radiated through my skull as I cupped my eye and began to cry.

"Oh, please. That barely hurt you."

I didn't respond. Falling the rest of the way to the floor, I cupped my eye and hoped he'd just leave. Letting out a heavy sigh, he got down, still in his towel, and put his hand on my shoulder. "I'm sorry, honey."

Jerking my shoulder away from him, I replied, "Go away!"

He stood up and left.

John hurt me sober? Rising to my feet, I headed into

the half-bathroom across the living room and looked

into the mirror. My eye was blood red—he had

popped a blood vessel. Tears welled in my eyes as

my eyebrows furrowed in disgust.

Four days wasn't soon enough to leave—I was

leaving today.

Did you enjoy this free sample?

Find it on Amazon.com!

OTHER BOOKS

Diamond Lake Series

One Thursday Morning (Book 1)

One Friday Afternoon (Book 2)

One Saturday Evening (Book 3)

One Sunday Drive (Book 4)

One Monday Prayer (Book 5)

One Tuesday Lunch (Book 6)

One Wednesday Dinner (Book 7)

Embers & Ashes Series

Amongst the Flames (Book 1)

Out of the Ashes (Book 2)

Up in Smoke (Book 3)

After the Fire (Book 4)

Love's Enduring Promise Series

The Perfect Cast (Book 1)

Finding Love (Book 2)

Claire's Hope (Book 3)

Dylan's Faith (Book 4)

Stand Alones

Love Again

Love Interrupted

A Chance at Love

The Lost Truth

Visit www.tkchapin.com for all the latest releases

Subscribe to the Newsletter for special

Prices, free gifts and more!

www.tkchapin.com

ABOUT THE AUTHOR

T.K. CHAPIN writes Christian Romance books designed to inspire and tug on your heart strings. He believes that telling stories of faith, love and family help build the faith of Christians and help non-believers see how God can work in the life of believers. He gives all credit for his writing and storytelling ability to God. The majority of the novels take place in and around Spokane Washington, his hometown. Chapin makes his home in the Pacific Northwest and has the pleasure of raising his daughter with his beautiful wife Crystal. To find out more about T.K. Chapin or his books, visit his website at www.tkchapin.com.

Made in the USA
Columbia, SC
01 April 2024

33869298R00190